Praise for Wind-of-Fire

"Wind-of-Fire is must reading for anyone who desires an inside view of the mind of the animal rights advocate. It radiates the pathos of a human being of great sensitivity who has given her life to advocating and interpreting a spirituality that human and nonhuman animals may share. It is a foundation document that will engender lively discussion and debate."
— **Douglas Stange, author of** *British Unitarians Against American Slavery and Patterns of Antislavery among American Unitarians, 1831-1860*

"Wind-of-Fire is an important book because it brings into focus a viewpoint sadly neglected in our society – a fascinating story."
— **Donna Read, Director of** *Goddess Remembered*

"Praise that Joan lives to peek into all our mirrors. This book, with its unique, superb, tongue-in-cheek humor, will move many and bring human consciousness and unconsciousness to another place!"
— **Connie Salamone, Women and Animal Activist Archive**

"If anything, the criticisms of traditionalist religion's disregard of the nonhuman creation are understated in Wind-of-Fire. Brilliant and original, Wind-of-Fire is an immensely readable work, profoundly mystical and down-to-earth."
— **Douglas Adams, Professor of Christianity and Arts, the Pacific School of Religion and Graduate Theological Union, Berkeley, California and author of** *Transcendence With The Human Body In Art*

"I was moved by 'Wind-of-Fire.' Your account of your relationship is insightful and witty."
— **Sy Safransky, Editor of** *The Sun, A Magazine of Ideas*

WIND-OF-FIRE

Related work by the Author

Creature Rites: Towards a Life Affirming Liturgy,
*M.A. thesis, unpublished, available through the
Graduate Theological Union Library, Berkeley, CA.*

WIND-OF-FIRE

The Story of an Untouchable

Joan Beth Clair

Wind-of-Fire Press
Berkeley, California

FIRST EDITION

Library of Congress Cataloging-in-Publication Data
Clair, Joan Beth
Wind-of-Fire: The Story of an Untouchable
Joan Beth Clair - 1st ed., 1999

ISBN 0-9635834-0-9

1. Animals -Religious aspects - Christianity. 2. Nature - Religious Aspects. 3. Animals, Treatment of. 4. Animal rights activist - Autobiography. 5. Sex discrimination against women. 6. Race discrimination. I. Title.

DEDICATION

For Wind-of-Fire, who "died for our sins."

Contents

Contents

Acknowledgments

Thanks to Saiom for her poems and Connie Salamone for her reading of an early version of the manuscript. Thanks to Carol Adams and Kathleen Fenton for their suggestions, and special thanks to Stanley McNail (a poet for the animals, who recently passed on) for proofreading a final version of the manuscript. Thanks to Dave Ampola, Mark Hillis, Rose Lernberg, Mindy Savory, Jeff Svare and Todd Takaki for providing some technical support in the production of this book. Special appreciation to Rose Evans for going over the final pages of the manuscript with me in preparation for publication, and thanks to John Evans for his helpful input.

In the course of this book, so as not to interrupt the flow for the reader, I have quoted some authors without giving complete citations in the text. More complete information for these quotations is as follows. Genesis 1:26 (p.7) is quoted from the Oxford version of the *Old Testament*, New York: Oxford University Press, 1973. The quotation from Barbara Berger (p.20) is from *Animalia*, Milbrac, California: Celestial Arts, 1982. The quotation from J. Allen Boone (p.25) is from *Kinship with All Life*, San Francisco: Harper, 1976. The quotation from Doris Day (p. 27) is from *Doris Day: Her Own Story* by A.E. Hotchner, New York: Bantam Books, 1975. The discussion of the events that took place concerning the bears in Yellowstone National Park (p.29) is based on *The Way of the Grizzly,* Dorothy Hinshaw Patent, author, New York: Clarion Books, 1987. The quotations from Barbara Woodhouse (p.34) are from *No Bad Dogs,* New York: Simon & Shuster, 1982 and *Dog Training My Way*, New York: Berkeley Books, 1983. The quotation from Farley Mowat (p.53) is from *Never Cry Wolf,* New York: Dell, 1973. The quotations from Jonathan Swift (p.54) are from *Gulliver's Travels,* Boston:Houghton Mifflin, 1960, Louis A. Landa, editor. The quotation from Dick Sutphen (p.85) is from *You Were Born Again to Be Together,* New York: Pocket Books, 1976. The quotation from St. Bonaventure (p.88) is from "The Life of St. Francis," E. Gurney Salter, translator; *The Little Flowers of St. Francis,* New York: E.P. Dutton, 1951. The quotation from Gandhi (p.90) is from *Gandhi's Autobiography: The Story of My Experiments with Truth,* Washington D.C.: Public Affairs Press, 1965. The quotation from Marija Gimbutas (p.115) is from *The Language of the Goddess,* San Francisco: Harper & Row, 1989. The quotation from Dane Rudhyar (p.119) is from *The Astrology of Personality,* New York: Doubleday, 1970.

Thanks to all who have supported a ministry for anima/ls over the years. Among them are Douglas Adams, Ellen Bring, Bob Brown (a divine minstrel for the animals), John Doud, Charles Emmons, Fred Fierstein, Durwood Foster, Allison Gold, Marsha Gravitz, Margaret Heard, Mary Heath, Gerald Jones, Mark Juergensmeyer, Elliot Katz, Pat Lennox, Charles McCoy, Eric Mills, Barbara Petrowiack, Pat Runo, Steven Sapontzis, Dona Spring, Muhaima Startt, John Stockwell, Florence Wallack, Ken White, Helen Zunes and the many people I have corresponded with over the years, throughout the United States and abroad, who encouraged this work.

Thanks, above all, to Moon, my anima/l companion of many years (who recently returned to his eternal home) for his uplifting spirit and all my other anima/l friends, past and present, who have been my teachers.

Author's Note

This book is the story of an untouchable: Wind-of-Fire. It contains the daily experiences I shared with Wind-of-Fire while attending seminary in Berkeley, California. These experiences woke me up to the fact that animals are untouchables in our society and that segregated attitudes towards animals ultimately result in alienation from ourselves.

It's a book about a woman and her dog.

It's also a book about finding one's self, the self that has been lost because it has been identified with the "animal;" anima/l, actually, as the word animal comes from the word anima, a word for the soul, the psyche and "the feminine."

Therefore, this is also a book about awakening or re-awakening into anima/l consciousness. This is a story about how one woman made that transition by getting in touch with the untouchable or anima/l within herself.

This book is written for all those who have felt alone because of their love for another form of life. This book is written particularly for those who, as children, were told that their animals wouldn't be there with them in heaven and who, as adults, were shamed and belittled for caring "too much" for their animal friends.

This book is also written for those who have left churches and other religious bodies because of the lack of acceptance of their animal friends, who were the same to them as family members.

This book is written for all those who have lost faith in the Supreme Mystery because of inhumanity towards other forms of life.

Wind-of-Fire's Morning Prayers

When dawn breaks, Wind-of-Fire rolls over on her back on the rug. She rolls from side to side, giving deep heaves of satisfaction. Then she goes over to the couch and rubs up against it like a cat. Then she comes over to the bed and nuzzles me. These are Wind-of-Fire's morning prayers. She says them like an asana* to the sun.

Through Wind-of-Fire I have learned a deep mystery, one that I could not understand through the Word alone. Through the Word alone I could not understand that life is a miracle, that I am a miracle and Wind-of-Fire a miracle.

One morning, after a night spent on the deep edge of despair, I woke up in a spirit of amazement. Wind-of-Fire was there, and she was totally vibrant and still. I understood through the Image the miracle of life.

---

*A hatha yoga exercise which is like a form of worship.

Translator of Wind-of-Fire

I accompany Wind-of-Fire at times as "translator." This took place the other day when I went inside a store on the other side of the University of California, Berkeley, campus.

Wind-of-Fire watches me with her usual enthusiasm. She puts her paws two inches too far into the terrain of the store interior. An imperious humanoid* appears from somewhere and "barks" at her like an "unruly animal" to get out. It is the right of every humanoid to tame the "wild" wherever it appears.

I assist the humanoid in taming the "wild beast" who has entered the store's interior two inches too much. Without nets, ropes, sirens and clubs we manage to get her outside.

---

*When I use the term "humanoid" instead of human, as I do in this book, I am trying to give the reader a sense of what it is like to be depersonalized, to be regarded as "thingness." When we treat others as if they are an inferior group, species or form of life, we lose the spiritual qualities that the word human suggests, qualities of humaneness and kindness. We act in an unconscious, programmed or automatic way, more like a robot, or humanoid, than a human being.

Wind-of-Fire continues to wait patiently. Apparently the humanoids sense the harmlessness of the "wild beast" and their faces relax. One smiles. Then both smile.

"Why don't you tie her up?" one wants to know.

"Because that would make her vulnerable," I answer. "Tied-up dogs have been known to disappear. There have been cases where they have reappeared in a vivisectionist's* laboratory."

---

*Vivisection means the cutting of a living animal in an experiment which causes the animal pain and suffering. A vivisectionist is a scientist who performs these experiments.

Walk with Wind-of-Fire

We were walking peacefully through a square when, all of a sudden, I hear an angry, squalling humanoid shouting at Wind-of-Fire. I notice she is eating some crusts of bread that are scattered on the sidewalk. I run up to her and pull her away.

The bird feeder is flailing his arms and yelling in a voice that would go over well in an audience of thousands. But there is just Wind-of-Fire and me and the crusts of bread and him in this square with some toasted leaves on the sidewalk and not a bird in sight.

I let him know I don't want Wind-of-Fire to eat the crusts of bread. I am dragging Wind-of-Fire away by her leash. The bird feeder continues to yell and flail his wings, or arms, like a huge bird of prey. Is he, perhaps, trying to make up karma from a prior incarnation as a vulture and I am interfering with his process?

I say, "I am taking her away; she is not eating your birds' bread."

Amazed at the degree of venom and hostility he is projecting, he stops. His voice comes back to him like an echo from a canyon. Its sharp edges stand up in empty space. He looks embarrassed.

May more humanoids hear their angry, insane voices yelling at the "untamed animals" of their own selves.

4

Tie Her to a Fence

It's a cool day; the wind is cleansing. I feel I have more space around me. It's a good day for a long walk with Wind-of-Fire.

On the other side of the University of California, Berkeley, campus, on Telegraph Avenue, the street is overcrowded and full of pizza scraps. Here I run into a friend. We decide to go to the University Art Museum's patio. My friend goes for tea. Wind-of-Fire sits near me. She is on a leash.

A man with a club walks up. He orders Wind-of-Fire out. "No dogs here. You can tie her to a fence."

Wind-of-Fire, tied to a fence, is still in sight. The leash is short. She can't sit down. "What did I do?" she communicates.

We finish drinking our tea quickly, claim our "untouchable"* and leave, having unwittingly violated the ritual purity of the place.

---

*When I use the term "untouchable," an exact analogy between those called "untouchables" in India and nonhuman animals is not intended. The analogy is used to stimulate another dimension of awareness.

Happy Hour

There is a "happy hour" outside the bookstore of the seminary* today. As we walk by, Wind-of-Fire is thrown a chip and then another. The humanoids laugh and admire the fact that Wind-of-Fire can catch the chips while they are in the air.

She misses one and bumps her head on a chair. One of the humanoids looks sorry. They want to know if I want anything to eat.

---

*While most of this book was being written, I was attending seminary in Berkeley, California.

The Dominion Effect

*"Then God said, 'Let us make man in our image,
after our likeness; and let them have dominion
over the fish of the sea, and over the birds of the
air, and over the cattle, and over all the earth,
and over every creeping thing that creeps upon
the earth.' "*
- Genesis 1:26

"... benedicamus Domino, 'let us bless the lord.' "

Perhaps the "Good Teacher" thought if young humanoids
(for after all, humanoids aren't very old) were given
"dominion" over the other creatures, they would have so
much self-esteem they would treat other creatures with
kindness and respect. If such were the plan, it evidently
backfired. Instead, those given the "authority" to protect and
respect saw themselves as superior to all other creatures. The
dominion effect, rather than restraining the hands of bullies,
created a class of tyrants who oppress and exploit other
creatures. They do not bless the Lord as they do not cherish
the blessing the creation is.

What an idea of God humanoids must have to believe that
when they are dismembering or supporting the dismembering

of other forms of life they are acting in the "image of God." God, the Vivisector?

As Gerald Jones and Scott Smith put it, in their book *Animals and the Gospel* (Thousand Oaks, Calif.: Millennial Productions, 1980): *"The idea that extreme cruelty is necessary to maintain human health makes a monster of God and is the 'end justifies the means' philosophy of gain that is the hallmark of Satan. The spirit of prayer, love and mercy is completely contrary to it."*

On the other hand, even conservative humanoids have been liberal in the interpretation of Genesis 1:26, giving permission to humanoids to dominate many of their own species, as well as the fowl of the air, the fish of the sea, the cattle and the earth.

Animals and Allergies

Before bringing Wind-of-Fire into the meeting, I ask if any of the women present object. Though I do not question that many people, including animal lovers, are genuinely allergic to nonhuman animals, it is my guess that we are living in a country in which more people are allergic to domestic animals than in most other countries of the world, though I don't quite understand why.

Is it possible that we have a truly ethnic national disease? If so, we have missed a great unifying factor that might transcend racial consciousness and superiority based on the same. It would be interesting to trace the history of this "disease" in our country and in the world to discover when and where it originated. When and where was the first "allergic reaction" noted?

There would appear to be enough contaminants in our environment, created by humanoids, to make it unnecessary to include in the category of "environmental pollutants or hazards" nonhuman creatures. I had never thought of nonhuman animals as being "hazardous to our health" in the same manner as humanoid-created pollutants. Yet one church wanted to issue a warning to "environmentally sensitive" members of its congregation that animals might be coming into the sanctuary for a *Blessing of the Animals* service.

Animals are segregated on the basis of sanitation in America the way untouchables were segregated on the basis of their lack of cleanliness in India. Every group that has occupied the bottom levels of society has been considered in some manner or other "unclean." Allergies do much to reinforce the untouchable caste of animals in our society.

None of the women object, but I notice that not one hand or voice reaches out in welcome to the untouchable beside me. The conversation that is carried on over her head and mine is extremely polite. It would have to be, it is taking place so far off the ground. It is taking place from seats that have been raised far above the earth, "Mother Untouchable" to us all.

Untouchables are always on earth level. Touchables are always above the earth. They comprise the body politic - polite. The women's voices are modulated and clear. They are clean voices. The clothes that are being worn are modulated and clean as well. They are eminently touchable, sanitized and cleansed. The fingernails are long and well kept.

Long fingernails can be one of the greatest tools of socialization of women. They have been my downfall in the socialization process. One week I very proudly decided to grow long nails. For a month I took care of them. I got them to the point where they were moderately long, not claws. I have tremendous admiration for real claws like the ones Wind-of-Fire has. Once I grew my nails I became aware of the "hidden sorority" of long fingernails. I began meeting other "fingernails" instead of other women.

Well kept fingernails have the danger of giving a woman a

sense of propriety, respectability and mannerliness which ultimately involves a rejection of nature rather than an identification with nature. One's warfare with "Mother Matter" takes place in a constant effort to keep one's fingernails free of dirt, impenetrable to disorder and untidiness. In order to do this, one naturally stays away from activities that might make one "dirty." Delicate finger nails become one's mantra, or holy phrase. If the mantra were repeated or the prayer beads read, the holy phrase might read: *"Too clean to touch, too clean to touch, too clean to touch."*

Around a woman reciting this mantra, a man might feel slightly unclean. Through this mantra the filthy projected part associated with the lowered class status of women is thrown back onto men, with a vengeance sometimes.

Yet, this is a form of "untouchability" in reverse which separates women from the natural world. Ironically, some women mimic the animal world while at the same time expressing loathing and distaste for anything that is a real animal. Animals are sacrificed cruelly as a part of this process, particularly in the area of women's cosmetics. In the Draize Test the eyes of rabbits are burned mercilessly in the testing of cosmetics so that women can present a veneer of the untamed, mysterious, wildness of "Mother Matter." Household products, such as detergents, are also tested on the eyes of animals.

Women, Animals and Dirt

Wind-of-Fire is still a puppy when we visit Ann.* While Ann and I are talking in the living room, Wind-of-Fire disappears into the kitchen. Ann runs into the kitchen after her and comes back with an expression of distaste on her face. Wind-of-Fire has upset the contents of the kitchen's garbage container. My hands become the brisk and rigid edges of a broom. They sweep pieces of tinfoil and potato scraps back into their place. It is a distasteful situation.

Now, as I recollect this scene, I look up the meaning of the word "distaste" in the dictionary. The root meaning of "taste" also means "touch." The root meaning of "dis" is "away." Inherent in the word "distaste" is "untouchable," that which cannot be touched or should not be touched.

---

*Out of respect for the privacy of those involved, I have changed some of the names in the vignettes.

In 1970 a study was done on sex-role stereotypes.* The subjects of the study were 33 women and 46 men, all of whom were clinically-trained psychologists, psychiatrists, or social workers.

A majority of those subjects tested agreed that "neat habits" was a trait of the psychologically healthy female and "sloppy habits" a trait of the psychologically healthy male. In general, the male traits were considered healthier.

Could this be one of the reasons why some women seem to fear contamination by animals? Could animals be a threat to the foundation on which they have built their self-esteem?

One summer, in my early twenties, I am asked out by a man who has been told I am a "neat girl." The mother of a friend of mine confides in me. She says the future husband of my friend is lucky because my friend is very neat about the way she keeps her clothing in her bureau.

In my early twenties I dream I am creating babies out of the mud. The babies are my paintings.

In my growing up years I was called a "tomboy," a dubious "compliment." I missed out on a part of the socialization process involved in being raised as a "little girl," with its obsessive concern with tidiness. It was all right if my clothes got dirty and even torn. As a child, my body was always bruised somewhere as a result of my explorations and encounters with "Mother Matter."

When I identify with Wind-of-Fire more than with Ann's

---

*Broverman, I.K., et al, "Sex-role Stereotypes and Clinical Judgments of Mental Health," *Journal of Consulting and Clinical Psychology*, 1970, Vol. 34, No.1, 1-7.

distaste, I am identified with what has been called the "masculine." Some of the little girls who gossiped about me when I was growing up, for not being the equivalent of "ladylike," have now grown into the respectable women who look with disdain on my love and relationship with Wind-of-Fire.

George Sand, considered by many of her contemporaries one of the greatest writers of the nineteenth century, was criticized for her "unclean" and "unfeminine" ways. Yet, perhaps, these were the very qualities that contributed to her genius.

Would women be expected to be so neat and clean, twice as neat and clean as men, if they weren't believed to be so dirty to begin with?

Witches and Brooms

Reflections on women, animals and dirt would not be complete without some mention of witches and brooms. The witch, or powerful wisewoman, who would have been burned at the stake a few centuries ago, becomes a cartoon strip. In "Broom Hilda," we had the ultimate portrayal of a woman who comes on too strong with men, a pushy hag. (A powerful woman cannot be a beautiful one.) Kitchen witches are sold in gift shops.

The actual tradition of women healers, who worshipped the Goddess and were members of indigenous religions in Europe and elsewhere, is a distorted memory in our popular culture where "witches" surface as hags at Halloween and the word "witch" is used as an insult. The fact that the religion of women (and men) labelled as "witches" was considered heretical by Christian zealots, in the same manner that the Native American religious traditions were branded by Christians, is accepted as true by many of today's scholars.

Think of the image of a witch on a broom! The broom was actually a symbol of a wand in the old religious traditions, a symbol of fire (spirit), one of the four elements. Limited to cleaning the domestic sphere, the wand becomes a broom. The power of creation inherent in the wand, a symbol of fire and spirit, is limited for women to the act of giving birth to human children in the home.

15

Ironically, it is believed that in the ancient matriarchal traditions, the protection and nurture of all creatures was a sacred role of the Goddess.* This is different from the patriarchal traditions which have attempted to make women a captive of the domestic sphere.

What is a witch on a broom doing flying through the sky? Is this a jailbreak, a role break, a reclaiming of the passion of the wand, the freeing of the spirit, a following of the spirit's fire?

---

* In the narrative that follows, I use the term goddess variously to refer to the Goddess of the older religious traditions and the Great Mother; as an expression for the Feminine or female aspect of the Divine; to refer to both the male and female aspects of the Divine, as in *God/ess*.

Patriarchy, Animals and Dirt

"I'm trying to understand why we're so concerned about cleanliness in this country," I say to a social psychologist at the university. " Animals are segregated from us, not allowed in stores, not allowed to be with us on public transportation. They're not segregated this way in many European countries. Why do we think of sharing public spaces with them as such a threat? Could there be any connection between the obsession with sanitation and attitudes towards animals?"

The social psychologist said it wouldn't surprise him if some studies had been done associating the obsessive-compulsive character type, associated with many "successful Americans," with a low level of tolerance or even dislike for animals. It takes this type of personality to succeed in the kind of society we live in, he went on to say.

If a whole society is obsessively concerned about the cleanliness of a certain group and the group is measured on the basis of cleanliness first, rather than other qualities, then the gas chambers aren't far away. Perhaps this is why animals are treated so badly in our country. The analogy is often made that vivisection is not different from the experiments that were performed on the Jews in Nazi Germany and the African American slaves.

The Jews were called an unclean race. They were considered inferior and segregated from the clean race, which was said to have a purity they lacked. They were forced into experiments for the benefit of the sanitized. Prior to the civil war, African American people, whose darker skin color gave them a more immediate identification with the earth (distorted into negative projections of dirt and lack of worth), were also experimented on. Millions of "dirty, inferior" animals suffer a terrible fate every day in laboratory experiments in America. Holocaust is a daily reality to them.

Mahatma Gandhi considered vivisection the worst of all crimes that human beings were committing on the face of the planet. In his autobiography, *The Story of My Experiments with Truth,* we discover he felt he had not purified himself sufficiently to be the leader of a movement to liberate nonhuman animals. Gandhi, who did much fasting, was concerned with inner purification and "cleanliness." How different our world might be today if we were more concerned with this inner form of "cleansing."

"Untouchables" usually are on the bottom of the socioeconomic ladder. And yet animals, in reality, own nothing at all. I thought of this the other day when I saw a dog, who probably had been abandoned, killed by a car on the freeway. She was a yellow dog and could be described as part shepherd and husky. She had no tags. She literally had nothing. Domestic animals in our society literally have nothing if they don't have the care of compassionate and loving people. All the dog had was the yellow body God had given her, valuable enough to be rendered into parts, the fate of unwanted, dead animals, when she was picked up by the highway patrol. I hope the dog's spirit will take the name I gave her, *Sunheart*, as I prayed goodbye.

It is the neglect of spirit that we will all be held responsible for in the end, whether the spirit is of a human or an animal body.

Anima/l

> *"Breath, life and soul were known as 'anima' in Latin. Our word 'animal' comes from this. There are always people who live in harmony with* Animalia ... *Many have been saints and sages who live in legend still."*
> — Barbara Berger

Anima is also a term for the Feminine. When we abuse, destroy and torture animals, we are destroying the anima/l within. When we treat animals as if they are without souls, we deny the anima/l, soul within ourselves. Whether we see this as Christ who is not being recognized in the form of an animal, or the Feminine that is being degraded, the results are the same. We live, as a result, in a world that does not reflect the Divine, because we have lost the relationship to the Divine as reflected in all creatures.

Sculptures of the Goddess, discovered from Neolithic times and earlier, show her sitting on a throne, or standing on a mountain, flanked by felines. Sometimes the Goddess has her hand on the head of a leopard or a lioness. It is as if she is drawing power from her anima/l, soul. In the ancient matriarchal religious traditions which worshipped the Goddess, all forms of life were considered children of the Goddess.

When Christianity persecuted those who practiced the old religious traditions, they saw a close relationship between a woman (or man) and a nonhuman animal (particularly cats) as evil. They labeled the people witches and their animals, "familiars." Yet the true familiarity of those who retained these ancient religious traditions was the knowledge that animals have souls. They retained their ability to see the spirit of other creatures. Native Americans and many indigenous peoples still have this respect and "familiarity" with other forms of life.

Unduly Concerned Animal Lovers

One way to find out that nonhuman animals are a class of untouchables is to treat them as if they aren't. Loving animals too much means treating them as if they are as worthy as humans. However, it is respectable to be an animal lover within limits. Perhaps *unduly concerned animal lover* is the phrase we are looking for.

Unduly concerned animal lovers have been characterized as little old ladies who "anthropomorphize" animals. I have never heard men parodied in this way, although they may love their animal friends as much. Inherent in the characterization of the bond between little old ladies and animals is the assumption that there is something abnormal if one is not a little old lady and still has a very close bond with a pet.

Likewise, there is some sympathy for a child having a close relationship with an animal. But often it is expected that the child give up this relationship when he or she matures. There is a sense that the bonds children form with animals are substitutes for relationships with human beings. At a certain point a child may be expected to "outgrow" a close bond with an animal companion.

A minister I know told me that many ministers reflect that the first memorial services they gave were for pets they had lost as children. However, the minister definitely gave me the idea that giving memorial services for adults who had lost companion animals was something these ministers didn't do. To give such a service might reflect *undue concern* or involvement.

In this we see a way of thinking which involves competing interests and hierarchy. In other words, if one has close involvements with other human beings, then one cannot or should not have a close involvement or attachment to an animal. If one has a close involvement with or attachment to an animal, this somehow threatens human relationships. In fact, the latter might be the case. There are many humans who will not give up or compromise their bonds with their animal companions for human relationships. They do not see their animals as expendable.

Unduly concerned animal lovers might buy old curtains out of a thrift shop that their cat can tear up to solve the problem of the cat clawing "good drapes." The fact that the cat, or dog, climbs on the furniture and may leave hair is something to be dealt with, with a vacuum cleaner. They don't give away the cat or dog at the first sign of some sort of behavioral difficulty, such as an indoor cat that begins to spray. They accept the good and the bad with their animal companion, the same way they would with a human companion, loved one or friend. The animal becomes a member of one's family. One does not give away a family member, especially a vulnerable family member like an animal who is dependent on one like a child.

There are many people who cook food for their animals rather than feeding their animals out of cans or bags of dry food. Sometimes they may do this because their animal has a medical problem and needs a special diet. They may also take out health and accident insurance for their pets. Perhaps it is only veterinarians and people who work in shelters who see the extent of the abuse of animals, who can appreciate this degree of *undue concern* for a "mere animal."

Mother Teresa said she saw Jesus in the lepers. When she served people with leprosy, she was serving Jesus. Seeing the Divine Mystery in animals and treating them with respect is honoring the Mystery that created them.

When women fought for inclusive language, (the use of "he" and "she" to denote gender, rather than the "generic he"), they were accused of having had bad experiences with their fathers, husbands and men. The implication was that they were somehow abnormal. Normal women wouldn't be concerned about the issue. And it was inferred that normal women had good relationships with fathers, husbands and men.

According to one organization which works to prevent family violence, an American woman is battered every nine seconds. It seems there are a large number of "abnormal women" in our society. It also appears that it is "normal" for a large number of young girls to be sexually abused by their fathers.

In a similar manner, *unduly concerned animal lovers* have been slandered for their loyalties to animals. They must have had bad experiences with other humans. That is the only thing that could account for their *undue concern*. The implication is that only abnormal humans could have bad experiences with others of their species. Yet even the *Old* and *New Testaments* of the Jewish and Christian traditions have passages in which we are urged to put our faith in God, rather than people.

As J. Allen Boone says in his book *Kinship With All Life:*

> *Men and women everywhere are being made acutely aware of the fact that something essential to life and well-being is flickering very low in the human species and threatening to go out entirely. This 'something' has to do with such values as love...unselfishness...integrity... sincerity...loyalty to one's best...honesty... enthusiasm...humility...goodness...happiness... fun. Practically every animal still has these assets in abundance and is eager to share them, given the opportunity and encouragement.*

There are hospital programs that have noted that only as a result of giving pets to patients have some patients improved and recovered. Why don't humans have the healing effect on their own species that animals have?

The belief that humans are the most capable of love is a speciesist illusion. *The American Heritage Dictionary of the*

English Language, third edition, (Boston: Houghton Mifflin, 1992), defines *speciesism* as "Human intolerance or discrimination on the basis of species, especially as manifested by cruelty to or exploitation of animals." Humans who respond with discomfort to evidence of a "familiar" (family) relationship between a human and animal may not be facing their own inability to give and receive love fully.

Some of the insinuating remarks I got while living on the grounds of the seminary with Wind-of-Fire had a sexual connotation. One seminarian, in particular, made jokes about "making out with dogs in the bushes." Some male humanoids, witnessing a close human-animal bond, may have reason to feel uncomfortable. Perhaps such a bond reminds them of pornographic "stag movies" which exploit women and animals. Perhaps such a bond makes them uncomfortable because of their own, past or present, exploitation and misuse of animals which they have not come to terms with.

Kindly humans might elevate your relationship with an untouchable to human status. "Oh, so she's a 'people dog,' " such a one might say.

Yet there are many humans who are willing to bear the stigmatization of caring "unduly" for an animal friend. I met one who worked for the University of California, Berkeley. He kept his dog with him in his office all day. He knew he was violating the "ritual purity" of the building, as I was by bringing Wind-of-Fire along with me when I visited his office. He was a married man whose wife worked, and he didn't think it was fair to leave his animal alone all day long.

I've known other people who have managed to bring their animals to work with them. The work atmosphere seems to improve as a result of the animal's presence.

However, one woman, who wanted to bring her dog to church with her, on occasion, was told by the minister that the dog might frighten members of the congregation. "Well I've been raped twice," the woman said, "Does that mean no men should be allowed in church because they would frighten me?"

Doris Day , the movie actress, says dogs "... have taught me how to be serenely patient, and they have taught me about love – fundamental love, such as Jesus taught."

When so many rules and regulations in our society limit our contact with animals and our capacity to care for them, actions that push these limits may seem excessive and *unduly concerned* at first. It is the limits themselves that are excessive. We have been cut off from much that is good within ourselves through being segregated from other forms of life.

Shambhala and Wind-of-Fire

I decided to talk with some of the people at Shambhala Bookstore in Berkeley to try to discover why they are so much more tolerant of "untouchables" than the average city storekeeper.

When I first came to Berkeley in 1980 from Chapel Hill, North Carolina, I called Shambhala Bookstore to find out if I could bring Wind-of-Fire into the store. In Chapel Hill, some of the storekeepers let animals in their stores. Instead of crowding two separate walks into an already overcrowded day, it would be nice to combine a Sunday afternoon walk with Wind-of-Fire with spending some time in Shambhala. The response of Shambhala was that it would be fine to bring her along, as long as she was well-behaved.

"Most storekeepers complain about fleas or complications," I say. "How do you deal with this?"

"Well, we do get fleas," one of the Shambhala people replied. "But it doesn't happen often."

"Or," I continued, "They complain that the animals won't behave."

"Well, when one doesn't we put the animal out," was the response. "We also have to put people out sometimes."

However, they wanted me to make it plain that this was not the store policy. They simply did not have a "negative policy" regarding pets.

Bears, Homicide and Rape

Some years ago there was a radical change in the policy towards grizzly bears in Yellowstone National Park. Bears and humans had coexisted peacefully. They passed each other in the common areas, and humans were never attacked by the bears. A lot of the bears fed off the food thrown away in the garbage dumps.

Members of the National Park Service believed that, with the increase of the tourist population, the bears might pose a hazard to humans. From 1968 to 1971, the dumps were phased out. The recommendations of two naturalists, the Craigheads, to provide the grizzlies with food during a transition period were ignored.

Once the dumps were closed, the hungry bears wandered into nearby campgrounds. A camper was killed by a grizzly in 1971, the first such death in 30 years.

As a result, the efforts to remove the bears from the former garbage dump and campground areas were escalated. In this process 189 bears were killed from 1968-1973, paying the price for the death of one human who was killed by one bear.

At least the bear did innocently what humanoids prefer to do covertly or in a premeditated manner under cover of darkness.

In a study done at N.Y.U. on anonymity and aggression, it was discovered that when a group of coeds had hoods on which protected their identities, they administered more shock to other coeds. When they didn't have hoods on and could be identified, they didn't give as much shock.*

It would have been interesting to compare how many homicides and rapes by male humanoids took place during the same time period in our nation's parks, had anyone cared to compare the statistics. Likewise, it might have been worth exploring how many men paid for the deeds of their "brothers," if these "brothers" paid the price at all.

Many deaths of bears, however, were not too many to avert the possibility of one more "human death." Untouchables are not judged on a one-by-one basis. The key factor was that a nonhuman animal had dared to harm a member of a superior species. The fact that humanoids mercilessly slaughter, torture, mutilate and vivisect millions of animals is taken as a matter of course, not "murder," but "manifest destiny." No doubt the lynchings in the south had a similar basis, the many paying for the alleged misdeeds of a few.

In terms of prediction, one would be on statistically firmer ground if one predicted violent behavior on the part of male humanoids towards women, than violent behavior on the part of bears. If men who raped women were treated as harshly as the bears, the safety of women would increase with far more reliability.

---

*Philip G. Zimbardo, "The Human Choice: Individuation, Reason & Order vs. Deindividuation, Impulse & Chaos," *Nebraska Symposium on Motivation*, U. of Nebraska Press, 1969.

However, from a speciesist standpoint, even the "lowliest" humanoid is to be judged individually. This is true theoretically, whether or not it is carried out in practice. Untouchables have few if any laws to protect them in theory or practice. And the ones they have are often unenforced. All untouchables are held accountable for the misdeeds of the few.

The Other Side of Pet is Pest

Nine year old Dica, who is a downstairs neighbor with cats, came to the meeting, at the seminary today, organized to determine whether pets should continue to be allowed in student housing. As we left the meeting Dica said, "Pets - pests, that's all I hear, pets - pests."

She was right on target. From pet control we are one step away from pest control. The other side of pet is pest. Pets are pests without the initial "s." When we go from pet to pest we are talking within the realm of extermination of one kind or another.

The Reverend Dr. Andrew Linzey discovered this in his efforts to protect the rabbits that had gone from pet to pest status on the grounds of the university where he taught in Great Britain. In Richmond, California, a movement formed, led by In Defense of Animals, to prevent the extermination of squirrels that people were feeding near a public swimming pool. Once again, a group of animals, in this case squirrels, went from pet to pest status.

Pets become pests when they are "too much trouble." They are too much trouble in ways we would never dream of considering humanoids too much trouble, unless they are a member of a group that has lower status such as women and African-Americans. Perhaps this is why no one complained about the many beer cans that rained down from the roof during a party in student housing at the seminary. Or the noise late into the night.

Women have a history of going from pet to pest status. A "good woman" knew how to remain a pet. She did not make "demands," become a pest. She was not too "pushy" - "pesty."

A dog or a cat in its place is a good dog or cat. Pets are indulged. Pests are exterminated. The fact that women and animals are untouchables is clear in the extermination of "witches"[women] and their "familiars" [animals] in the Middle Ages. Both were regarded as a pestilence.

The Segregation of Animals

The segregation of animals becomes clear in public places. Domestic pets are barred from eating places, restaurants and food stores because of "health measures" and fear of contamination in America. These sanitized measures have extended to institutions and places of business where no laws on the books ban animals based on sanitation or health. At the time I attended seminary with Wind-of-Fire until early 1985, even the Franciscan Seminary in Berkeley did not have a policy which would have made it permissible for Wind-of-Fire to enter the building. A portrait of St. Francis, the Saint of All Creation, hangs over a corridor trafficked only by humanoids.

This fear of "complications" posed by animals is not shared by at least two major European writers on animals. They suggest that pet owners treat their pets inclusively, as members of their families. Barbara Woodhouse, in *No Bad Dogs*, recommends that dog owners take their dogs with them wherever they go. In *Dog Training My Way,* she says: *"A holiday abroad is out of the question owing to quarantine regulations. To most of us dog lovers these restrictions are taken as a matter of course. The dog is part of the family and we wouldn't leave one of the family behind."*

James Herriot, in one of his books, describes getting a

haircut with his dog curled up beneath the barber chair. This is not possible in the Bay Area of California where the Board of Cosmetology, Department of Consumer Affairs, Regulation #971 spells out the rules for animals in haircutting places: *"Sanitation Requirements for Cosmetology Schools & Establishments ... No person shall bring any animal into, or permit any animal to remain in a school or establishment."*

Although Jesus was born among oxen and other animals in what might have been a well cared for part of the house, as peasants cared for their animals; it would be considered improper, in most churches, to bring animals along to celebrate the day of his birth.

Yet several years ago I attended a Christmas service in which there must have been at least five bawling humanoid children. Not one parent removed their child from the service, making the words of the minister inaudible to many. If an untouchable had attended, however well behaved, there could well have been an uproar – even more so if one had dared to bark or cry.

Knowing One's Place

When one is an untouchable, the slightest deviation from "propriety" appears to be outrageous. Rosa Parks refusing to take a back seat on a bus is a case in point. "Knowing one's place" is regarded as a positive attribute of an untouchable. The "good untouchable" knows its place the way members of minority groups, including women, were expected to know their place in former times and in many circumstances today.

I was told by an ex-farmer that he had a "farmer's mentality" towards animals. This meant that an animal had its place and "... if they get out of it, we wring their necks." When one begins to befriend untouchables in a way that violates the "ritual purity" of "their place," some humanoids might feel like wringing your neck too. Accustomed to thinking in terms of hierarchy, it disturbs their expectations of a "master-slave" relationship in regard to animals. After all, you are supposed to be the animal's "master," not its friend, and certainly not its advocate.

One night I attended a meeting. I asked the leader beforehand if I could bring Wind-of-Fire. I explained that Wind-of-Fire was a well-behaved dog.

The answer was, "No; it might be disruptive."

The night of the meeting arrived. I took a seat. I noticed that the seat next to me had some baby things on it. A moment later, we had the entrance of the leader's baby, led by the leader's wife. The *darling little humanoid* entered the circle and made some sounds which some thought were just delightful. The leader made some proud and pleased parent-type remarks. Throughout the meeting, the little humanoid continued to squeak and clatter around the room.

The discussion leader would not have understood if I had said, *"Your darling, little humanoid disrupted this meeting about a hundred times more than my dog would have, had I been permitted to bring her."* Untouchables and humanoids are not comparable. What is considered an outrageous breach of propriety on the part of one is considered a delightful "breach of propriety" on the part of the other.

Some would say Wind-of-Fire is an "exception" to blubbering, slobbering, boisterous "dogkind." [This is the same as saying that some girls did not fit into stereotypical images of girlhood or womanhood, were not "silly" or "empty-headed," the way young girls and women were once supposed to be.] I think there are many dogs like Wind-of-Fire. She knows that a frisbee is not a squirrel. She doesn't waste her time running after a piece of plastic. Like a Zen master she gets up when there's a reason to get up. Like a Zen master she lies down when there's a reason to lie down. She doesn't jump up and down frenetically. She runs when there's something to interest her, like chasing a squirrel. She doesn't jump up on strangers. In fact, she's dignified, discerning and wise.

Yet, on an average day, on an average stroll through the park, with Wind-of-Fire running a few paces ahead of me, behind me or to the side of me, I may hear, "Here, dog." It's as if every imperious humanoid is the natural owner of the "beast in the wild." The voices of these strangers are imperious and well-defined as if untamed and at large nature is being asked to "heel." These are the voices of people that I don't know and Wind-of-Fire doesn't know.

Let's say your two year old child is crawling around in the grass a few paces from where you sit. A stranger you don't know comes along and in an imperious voice says, "Here, child." More likely you'd think you were dealing with a child kidnapper than someone you felt had a right to order your child around. But it is different with animals. A "good dog" should obey any humanoid's command.

And the relationship that is understood here is about "commandments," about "training," about "obedience," not about interspecies communication, cooperation and love.

Patriarchy turns life into a performance. The female victims of this way of life "turn tricks." The animal victims are expected to perform them.

Dinner and Revolution

The dinner dynamics are stereotypical. We all seem oddly segregated from one another. The women talk about the food. The men talk politics. One of the women present asks me if I would like to exchange "bites."

Wind-of-Fire would like to exchange "bites" too. She's on the same side of the table as the other women and myself. However, she's not content to exchange "bites" with the women at the table. She wants a "bite" from the plate of the male humanoid across the table whose mouth is full of politics.

In a burst of revolutionary energy, upsetting the power dynamics of dining between women and men, she heaves her eighty pound body into the middle of the political interchange, an unrestrained energy without a slogan, an unformulated cause.

If a group of poor humanoids were tied to a table leg and had to watch a wealthier group of humanoids eat food in front of them that they were denied, and one of this group broke free and plunged into the middle of the table for a "bite," this would be regarded as either insanity or revolution.

Untouchables have their place in the politics of dining. Like the "black nannies" of old, they're expected to eat by themselves somewhere off in the kitchen, even if they're the most nurturing and faithful "member of the family." Their qualities are gratuitous. An untouchable has "its food." Its food is usually the remnants of other animals whose lives have been tormented and tortured, whose essence has been unappreciated and unloved.

Would one eat a full meal in front of a guest in one's home? Would one reserve the worst food for one's guest and eat a hearty meal in front of him or her? I remember a humanoid denying his dog any table scraps with pride. "She's not going to be a beggar," he said. I think of St. Lazarus, the beggar, portrayed with his dogs in Catholic icons. The dogs lick his wounds. Yet we do not see homeless persons or hounds as holy here in our country.

By asking to be treated like a human member of the family, the dog was "acting like a beggar." In denying the scraps, the dog was, in fact, being denied full family membership. If a human child were treated this way, we would say he or she was being treated like an animal. And in most cases that would be an apt description.

Not family members. Not guests. And don't beg to be treated as such. Is there some positive manner in which a dog has a right to be treated like a dog, a cat like a cat, a horse like a horse, an elephant like an elephant, a camel like a camel, a tiger like a tiger - in a way that does not violate their being, but does justice to their dignity as creatures of God?

When I first came to seminary I was told there was a vegetarian eating plan. As it turned out there was hardly any food that I could eat. The cook became indignant when I wanted to take home the meat for Wind-of-Fire. After all, I was paying for it. And if I couldn't eat it, at least Wind-of-Fire could. However, the cook was going to be sure that Wind-of-Fire didn't get any. When the cook wasn't watching, she had her assistant "chef" spy on me to be sure I wasn't taking any meat out of the dining room for Wind-of-Fire.

Eventually, all those who were dissatisfied with the eating plan, for various reasons, organized. Some of us managed to get excused from the plan. In the meantime, we got a new cook who had lived in a monastery and knew how to prepare vegetarian food.

Before these changes took place, however, the only outlet for my frustration was the outdoor barbecues when neither the cook nor her assistant were present. If anyone had told me I'd be "smuggling" home food I was paying for, for my dog, my first year at seminary, I wouldn't have believed them. Nor would I have wanted to feed her this food had I any idea, at the time, of the tremendous suffering of factory-farmed animals who become "meat."

Untouchable Food

Untouchable food is a million dollar industry. The food is advertised as healthy and nourishing, but it is the food that has been put together from the remains of animals who have not been respected or treated well while alive. This is also the case for the food human beings eat. Most of the meat, eggs, dairy products and milk that humans eat come from animals that have been treated in an abominable manner while they are alive. The untouchable is given the least desirable parts of these unloved, uncared-for animals.

Perhaps this knowledge remains within the "shadow" of the owners' of domestic animals. Domestic animals share in the spoils of other animals who have been abused. There, but for the grace of God, they too may go, into situations of abuse. They may be delivered to pounds, from which they can be sold into laboratories, once the "grace" of the human caretaker has been removed. They may end up on "death row" in an animal shelter, barking desperately each time a person walks by their cage.

So if not a guest, not a family member, a domestic animal's status is always a tentative one. The animal may be "tolerated," in spite of the fact that it is an animal. It is "spoiled" when it is given too much of the spoils that humanoids have at the expense of other creatures.

Groundless Relationships

I run into Dixie outside of a church in Berkeley. She is trying to get signatures for a petition which calls for halting experimentation on animals outside their natural habitats. This would end the slave trade of chimpanzees and other animals from the tropics.

In the time I am there with Dixie, only one member of the church stops at all. This humanoid, ignoring the literature, gives us a "piece of his mind." It is an angry "piece of mind," full of disapproval. Having given us this "piece of mind," which has no peace, he walks on.

Dixie and I are dressed casually. I think of casual dress as "earthward" dress, comfortable clothing that does not have to be controlled. Some of us wore clothing of this kind, meant for wear and tear, when we were children and young adults. The clothing had an innocence to it; it lacked the formality of "school dress." After school, we couldn't wait to get into our casual clothing, to get outdoors and play. We'd play basketball, punchball, volleyball and softball, or ride our bikes. The clothing enabled us to be active, to stretch our muscles and *be*, not *appear* a certain way. However, humanoids do not wear "earthward" clothing to church. And we stand out as the Christians in "heavenward" clothing pass us by.

43

After the last one passes by us, without acknowledging or showing any interest in the petition, Dixie and I sit on the ground. In fact, the three of us, Dixie, Wind-of-Fire and I sit in a circle. Like three squaws we squat.

I think of how literally groundless my relationship usually is to Wind-of-Fire. Perhaps the Native Americans felt closer to animals and nature than we do because they were not separated from other creatures by elevated chairs, tables and beds, which encourage a sense of segregation and superiority.

Humanoid eating, sleeping and socializing structures are heavenward structures, not earthward structures. They reinforce the idea of the untouchability of nonhuman animals. They create a sense of separation between "heavenward" (human) and "earthward" (nonhuman) creatures. Should an untouchable sit on a heavenward structure, it has violated ritual purity. The untouchables being referred to here are the domestic animals that share our lives. But a picture of a Buddhist monk with his arm around a reindeer shows them sitting on the ground. A picture of Krishna with his arm around a cow, shows them sitting on the ground as well.

Perhaps this form of segregation contributes to the reason why so many churchgoers could not stop to find out what was happening to the "earthward" creatures "beneath" them.

Born Into Christians

Sociologists have discovered that when one group is separated at random from two separate groups, each group assumes that it is the in-group and better than the out-group. To look at this from another angle, if you want humanoids to think they are better than other humanoids, divide them into groups, give each group a name, and give them symbols to represent the group they're members of. Sociologists call this phenomenon "mere differentiation." *

We do not have to go far today to discover "ritual purity" based on "mere differentiation." Many people who call themselves Christians relate to Christianity as an in-group of a class, ethnic, or "racial" group they have been born into as an accident of birth. Perhaps they should be called "born into" Christians.

Sociologists have discovered that people in the in-group see themselves as more variable and the out-group as less variable or heterogeneous. The act of "mere differentiation" may be enough to begin this process.

---

*Two articles about "mere differentiation" are as follows: Tajfel, "Experiments in Intergroup Discrimination," *Sci Amer*, Nov.1970, 96-102; Howard & Rothbart,"Social Categorization and Memory for In-Group and Out-Group Behavior," *Journal of Personality and Social Psychology,* 1980, Vol.38, No. 2, 301-310.

The riches of the soul are so deep, miraculous and extraordinary that having experienced one touch of the Divine Mystery, how can one return to narrow, stereotypical categories of understanding of the animals and humans on earth. How did the breadth of Paul's teaching, "there is neither male nor female, Jew nor Greek [and I would add, human nor animal] in Christ," get whittled down to such a narrow vision based on sexism and speciesism. Instead of knowing the richness of Christ, how did the sex of the body or the species of the "form" become all important? If anything, we can all claim, with some regret, to be members of the "human race" that has perpetuated all these divisions. Yet this is the "vision" born-into Christianity has settled for, a "racial faith tradition," within the tradition of patriarchal tribalism, rather than a truly religious one, and it isn't enough. It doesn't bring about the "kingdom/queendom" on earth.

Dogs, Dirt and the French

Ed, the guy who owns the Euclid Tennis Shop in Berkeley, has a dog named Aubrey.* Aubrey stays with Ed in the store all the time that the store is open. This is the way its been since Ed opened the store.

Aubrey occupies a space that would generally be considered ritually impure as a result of his presence there. He lies with his paws toward the door and customers frequently have to walk around him to get into the store's interior.

Ed's business is doing well. If athletes, of either sex, identify with the "masculine" in exposing themselves to "Mother Matter's" dirt, perhaps this accounts for the lack of allergic reactions to Aubrey. At any rate, Ed has never had a problem.

I ask Ed how it is that he seems to be able to manage with a dog in the store when most storekeepers won't let animals inside such "ritually pure" places.

"They do it in France," Ed replies.

"I've wondered about that," I say. "I've wondered why it is that in France they seem so much more relaxed about animals, germs, fleas, hair."

---

*Aubrey, God bless him, passed on since this was written, The Euclid Tennis Shop has closed.

"It's because they're so dirty in France," one of the customers in the store says. "The French are dirty; they even have outdoor pissoirs."

I think that when "Mother Matter" designed outdoor, French pissoirs she really hit the pits. She should have realized that cement doesn't need to be defecated on. She should have built outdoor French pissoirs out of earth and lined them with grass. In the "kingdom/queendom," as in the "garden of Eden," we will rediscover French pissoirs, the real, original French pissoirs, the way they were intended to be.

"I like dogs," Ed says. "They're all right by me."

Bank Cal's Pet Policy

Bank Cal has a promising, well lettered, conservative looking sign on the left-hand side of the door of its bank in Berkeley which says, "No unleashed dogs."

I decide to call the bank to discover how this place of business manages to work out all the "complications" that animals presumably present, a feat that even the Franciscan Seminary in Berkeley hasn't been able to achieve.

I notice as I go into the bank that there are rugs. The rugs are in the section where bank customers go to consult with bankers. Presumably "leashed dogs" are welcome there also.

The bank clerk who answers my telephone call explains that Bank Cal isn't Bank Cal anymore, but is now another bank. In that case, I ask, have all the personnel changed in the bank as well? "They have not," is the reply. "You probably want to speak with Mr. A.," the voice continues.

I am unable to contact Mr. A. for several days and finally reach him shortly before closing time one afternoon. I assure him, from the outset, that I am all for public places allowing people's pets. I want to ask him a few questions about how such a policy has arisen and been carried out by the bank. "I think it is wonderful that the bank permits dogs on leashes," I assure him.

"Do we have a policy that permits dogs into the bank?" Mr. A. wants to know.

"Well, yes, you do," I reply. "You have a large sign on the left-hand side of your door which says, 'No unleashed dogs.' I assume this means that leashed dogs are allowed."

"Well, yes, that is what one would assume," Mr. A. responds. "But I don't recall ever having seen such a sign. Where did you say the sign is located?"

I explain that the sign is located outside the door, and to the left of the door.

Mr. A. wants to know if the sign is outside or inside the bank.

At that point my unverbalized thoughts are running as follows: "How on earth should I know what side of the door the sign is on. It's your bank; don't you know what's going on in *your* bank?" But I say, "I'm sorry I cannot give you any more information. It's near the door."

Mr. A. asks me if it is all right if he goes and looks.

I say that will be fine.

Seconds go by, minutes. I am beginning to wonder if I have ever seen a sign outside the bank's door, when Mr. A. comes back.

"Well, I'll be darned. You're right. There is a sign by the side of the door. I've worked for this bank for over seven years, and I never noticed that sign before."

So much for the only business establishment in Berkeley with a public policy which allows "pets." [Since writing this, the sign has been removed.]

Do Men Have Souls?

The consciousness that many of us have towards animals is similar to the consciousness of men who befriended women when it was believed women did not have souls or souls equal to the souls of men. Although the equality or existence of women's souls may not be disputed today, still disputed is the equality of a woman's body. St. Paul said there is neither male or female in Christ. In other words, one cannot base one's identity on "maleness"or "femaleness" and be in Christ. As "maleness" is the basis of the Catholic priesthood, are they in Christ? Or, are they, and any other denomination with an exclusive male "priesthood," in a "holy boys club."

It is ironic that today many men will not acknowledge the existence of the "soul." Their actions are a form of "soul denial" as well. A soul is not a part of a "rational experience" of "reality" that many men are taught to identify with as an expression of their "manhood." It becomes rather difficult to see their soul at all. Theirs is a rather voluntary invisibility.

When the soul is denied, its qualities are not valued or understood. Humans who care about animals cannot understand how creatures, like dogs, who manifest qualities of unconditional love, selflessness, loyalty, nonjudgmentalness, compassion and spontaneity, can be vivisected in laboratories and abused. If these qualities of the soul were valued and

51

acknowledged, no one could treat these animals in this manner. The vivisectors would realize they were committing a sin against God.

Particularly men in our society are taught to value anti-soul qualities: qualities of indifference, uncaring, toughness, callousness, "neutrality," and "objectivity" [an expression for soul-denial].

Therefore, it is gratifying to find some men acknowledging the existence of a soul. One such man sat on an animal research committee. He told me that the committee had approved research on twelve golden retrievers, his favorite dog. He did not feel he could press for their release at that point, as he had just negotiated another measure that would spare some other animals suffering. It was the soulfulness of the animals, their gentleness and innocence, in the "psychic space" where the "soul" is, that hurt him. For the other committee members, that space was apparently empty.

The De-Speciesism Process

Farley Mowat, the author of *Never Cry Wolf* , had a rare opportunity to live among wolves for long stretches at a time in the arctic regions of Canada. He begins to appreciate the qualities of his animal neighbors:

> George was a massive and eminently regal beast
> whose coat was silver-white .... His dignity was
> unassailable, yet he was by no means aloof.
> Conscientious to a fault, thoughtful of others,
> and affectionate within reasonable bounds, he
> was the kind of father whose idealized image
> appears in many wistful books of human family
> reminiscences, but whose real prototype has
> seldom paced the earth upon two legs .... His
> wife was equally memorable .... I became deeply
> fond of Angeline, and still live in hopes that I
> can somewhere find a human female who
> embodies all her virtues.

Other authors have left records of their disillusionment with the "human" species and their growing appreciation of animals.

Jonathan Swift, Dean of St. Patrick's Cathedral, Dublin, in the eighteenth century, praises the wisdom of horses (the *Houyhnhnms*) in his book *Gulliver's Travels*. He sketches, by way of comparison, the *yahoos*, a race of degenerate humanoids. Responding to his critics, Swift in the guise of Captain Gulliver states:

> *And, it must be owned, that seven months were a*
> *sufficient time to correct every vice and folly to*
> *which yahoos are subject, if their natures had*
> *been capable of the least disposition to virtue or*
> *wisdom; yet so far have you been from answer-*
> *ing mine expectation in any of your letters, that*
> *on the contrary you are loading our carrier*
> *every week with libels, and keys, and reflections,*
> *and memoirs, and second parts; wherein I see*
> *myself accused of reflecting upon great*
> *statesfolk, of degrading human nature (for so*
> *they have still the confidence to style it)....*

Swift concludes that the *yahoos* are such a degenerate species that they are beyond redemption:

> *I must freely confess, that since my last return*
> *some corruptions of my yahoo nature have*
> *revived in me by conversing with a few of your*
> *species, and particularly those of mine own*
> *family, by an unavoidable necessity; else I should*
> *never have attempted so absurd a project as that*
> *of reforming the yahoo race in this kingdom; but*
> *I have now done with all such visionary schemes*
> *for ever.*

I was brought up in a city. On a trip to the country, when I was six or seven years old, I encountered farm animals for the first time. I remember feeling in awe of a calf tied to a fence. Looking into the calf's huge, brown eyes, I felt I was in the presence of the most beautiful creature I had ever seen. I felt the Divine in her. Her eyes were full of Love.

In retrospect, I understand how Hindus revere the cow. When the Hindu says, "I salute the Divinity in you," they include all species.

Perhaps Paul was thinking of the Divine when he said, in the *New Testament*, "See only the perfect man." With humanoids, however, it would not be necessary to emphasize seeing the "perfect part," if the other part weren't so blatantly obvious.

When one goes through the de-speciesism process, it is possible to feel like Mowat and Swift. It is also easy to forget that oneself was also a speciesist in many ways before one's awareness awakened and that in daily life one has to fight to hold onto this awareness and live it out, once it has arrived. This is not easy, as there is always more to learn.

When someone asked me about the direction of my spiritual life, I told her that in recent years I felt I was growing spiritually through my relationship with Wind-of-Fire and my other anima/l friends. I said, "My whole life has been a quest for God/ess, a coming closer to God/ess, and right now I am considering the fantasy or idea of living with more animals, because I feel that would bring me more into harmony with the Divine."

The Anima/l Self

Farley Mowat says at one point that he hopes to find his anima/l self as a result of his trip to the arctic. He hopes that this will somehow make him into a new person.

As a woman I no longer feel separated from my anima/l self, but it took me years to reclaim it. I believe, in our society, many girls as well as boys, but not to the same extent, are brought up in a way which discourages them from expressing their feelings. I can remember crying only once between the ages of six and eighteen. Yet somewhere inside me I knew that living as if I didn't have feelings was one of the most horrible things I had ever experienced. I knew I had to find my way out of it.

I remember, as a teenager, standing on a street outside a movie theatre with some of my friends. A woman fell to the sidewalk in our presence. My friends and I were numb. But one woman in the crowd ran up to the woman compassionately. She was the only one to respond. I remember wanting to be like her, but I couldn't feel. It took me years to break out of this. My quest for the *holy grail* of feeling inside myself was more important to me than any form of outward success. Finally I could, on occasion, be like this woman. I could feel compassion for others. That was the greatest gift that was given to me, one I never want to take for granted.

If a part of the Creator is in each creature, then we are all a part of the anima/l or "animal self." When we violate any other creature, we violate ourselves and the Creator. We have taken the "left-handed" path the mystics talk about, of the mind separated from the heart. Whoever created the factory farms for animals was creating with a mind separated from the heart. Yes, these farms give enormous profits. They also reap tremendous suffering for humans and animals. Is it heart thinking to make cows into assembly line milking machines, to de-beak chickens and keep them crowded in cages their whole lives, to send them down conveyer belts? Is it any accident that the Jews were taken to the concentration camps in cattle cars?

Let's take a look at a factory farm in which mother pigs that give birth are squeezed between bars. Did the Creator create us to profit from their suffering? How much money have we put in Her bank, as a result of having been given the gift of life, through atrocities like these? Who are we to tamper with natural means of giving birth, or the birth giving process of Her creatures? If we cannot cherish the birth giving process of one form of life and treat nonhuman animals as reproductive machines, can we truly value or cherish life in any form?

Sacred Sow

Pigs were not always considered the lowest and dirtiest of the untouchables. Robert Sidwell makes the point that:

> *The pig at one time symbolized something quite*
> *at variance with the deep disgust that it conveys*
> *today; it symbolized the archetypal feminine,*
> *'the fruitful and receptive womb.' The pig was*
> *commonly depicted in the company of the Great*
> *Goddess in any number of her manifestations –*
> *Isis, Demeter, Cybele, etc. It was an animal so*
> *sacred that to partake of its flesh was taboo*
> *save during religious ceremonies, when it was*
> *consumed by celebrants. Perhaps even more*
> *shocking is the suggestion put forth by Frazer*
> *and others that originally this beast was the*
> *form of the Great Goddess herself, for the*
> *attendant animal of a deity betrays the original*
> *form of the deity.*
> ("On Pigs – Sacred & Chauvinistic,"
> *Anima, Six/2)*

Sidwell makes the startling observation that those animals that are most disliked by patriarchy are the very animals that were associated with the Goddess and the matrifocal world.

If one eats the flesh of an animal whose life has been made miserable as a result of human cruelty, even if one says prayers of thankfulness before one eats or apologizes to the spirit of the animal, what is one taking in on the level of one's own spirit?

Yellow Jade and Fire-Wind Dog

John Blofield was inscribing books he had written at Shambhala Bookstore today. When I told him the name of my dog, Wind-of-Fire, he called her "Fire-Wind Dog." He inscribed one of his books on Buddhism, which I purchased, as follows: "A Fire-Wind Dog is two-fifths on the way to enlightenment. May you, Joan, provide the other three- fifths."

I also told him about Yellow Jade. Before coming to seminary, I lived with Yellow Jade, Wind-of-Fire and Little Beast in Chapel Hill, North Carolina.

I have always felt that Yellow Jade reached whatever enlightenment was for her before she passed on.

"Yellow," Blofield said, "is the color of Buddhism; it is an auspicious color."

Neighbors said that Yellow Jade was the kind of dog that everybody wanted. Possibly this was because she, in retrospect, looked like and probably was a corgi. I didn't know much about breeds at that time, nor was she introduced as such when the woman from the local humane society brought her to me. Possibly everybody wanted her because she never made any disturbances of any kind. She barked only at the right times. She was perfect with children and other animals, including cats.

She always seemed to be immaculately clean. I don't remember Yellow Jade ever having one flea in all the months we lived together. She was a great protectress, great company and great fun. She was very independent, very affectionate and very loyal. We loved each other.

In the morning Yellow Jade would go outside and run in the woods and swim in a nearby stream. Then she'd come home for breakfast.

When I moved with Yellow Jade from our apartment, a block away from the woods, to an apartment right next to the woods, I sensed something was wrong. The new apartment didn't feel like the right place for Yellow Jade. Yellow Jade seemed to feel the same thing. When we looked at each other, we knew something was wrong.

At that time I had a young friend who also lived in the apartment complex. She became very friendly with Yellow Jade, and Yellow Jade came to trust her.

One night before Yellow Jade and I moved into the new apartment, I had a dream in which this young friend said, "Oh, Joan, I'm going to hurt you." She said this in a sad and mournful tone of voice.

Before moving into the new apartment, I had an intuition that on a certain day a few weeks hence there would be the danger of a car accident. I assumed the danger was to me. I had never had such a premonition before, and I didn't think about it again.

When the language of the "rational mind" became dominant, it denied all other forms of knowing apart from analytical and empirical knowledge. However, what has been called knowledge and insight cannot be discerned through the analytical mind alone. There is another "language;" it is at the heart of one's being. It can manifest in many ways - as clairsentience, clairvoyance, extrasensory perception, precognition. It is the language of the psyche, the intuitive, art, the feminine and mysticism. These forms of knowing have been judged, in a biased manner, as superstition or worse.

Intuitive knowledge is not linear, logical or conscious in the sense we ordinarily define consciousness. It was not linear or logical that one evening I said to Yellow Jade: "Yellow Jade, you're perfect. You're more perfect than me. You've been a wonderful friend, and I appreciate all you've done. You don't have to stay here any longer, if you don't want to. You're free."

It was the evening before the day I'd intuited might bring a car accident, but I'd forgotten this.

The next morning, about the time Yellow Jade usually came home, she did not appear. I waited all day for her, but no Yellow Jade. That night there was still no Yellow Jade. I ran into my young friend the next day and told her Yellow Jade hadn't come home.

"Oh, no, Joan, didn't you know?" she said.

"Know what?" I asked.

She told me that Yellow Jade had followed her on her way to school. She had run to catch the school bus; she had been late. She didn't turn around to bring Yellow Jade back home. At the intersection where the school bus stopped, just as she boarded, Yellow Jade had been hit by a car. My friend had not looked back. Yellow Jade's body was taken to the garbage dump.

This was the friend who had said in the dream, "Oh, Joan, I'm going to hurt you."

It was hard to know in what way I was more hurt - by the loss of Yellow Jade or by the way in which I lost her. I was hurt by the fact that her young friend and mine hadn't turned around and brought her back home, even if that meant she would be late for school. And I was even more hurt by the fact she hadn't stopped to find out if Yellow Jade was still alive after she'd been hit. We still remained friends after this happened, however.

That night, while I was asleep, Yellow Jade came to me in a dream. She was all white, radiant light.

Little Beast, Brown Beast, Wind-of-Fire and Lady

My mourning period was outwardly short for Yellow Jade.
I knew what I had to do immediately. I had to get another
dog. As it turned out, I got three. I found Little Beast on the
street without identifying tags. I got Wind-of-Fire from an ad
in the local newspaper when she was just three months old.
And the local pound dropped Lady off on a trial basis for
"just a few days."

All four of us walked up and down the block of the apartment
complex, and the neighbors panicked about the pee. Mornings
I was out on the sidewalk with a mop and pail removing all
traces of Wind-of-Fire's inability to control herself.

The neighbors, however, loved Lady. The name assured
them, I think, that there was some semblance of normality
going on with all these dogs.

What prejudiced me against Lady, however, the first day of
her arrival was an inexplicable gesture on her part in which
she appeared to be taking the side of Little Beast against me,
as if I was persecuting him. The problem was I hadn't done
anything to Little Beast. There were no sides to choose. Since
people project and transfer onto others what they're
unconscious of in dream and reality, perhaps she was doing

something similar with me. Possibly she was reliving something that had been done to her. However, at the time, I responded, "How could you imagine such a thing. I'd never do anything to hurt Little Beast. I love Little Beast." I said this emotionally, and Little Beast got upset in turn and licked my face.

At the other side of the apartment complex from where we now lived were an unusual family who became uncle, great-uncle and aunt to Wind-of-Fire and Little Beast. These neighbors, who lived in the apartment beneath the one I lived in before we moved, knew who Little Beast's human companion was because he was a friend of theirs. In fact, these neighbors were the "owners" of Brown Beast, after whom Little Beast had been named. Their friend had been working two jobs and two shifts and couldn't "keep the beast under control."

Little Beast, as it turned out, was of aristocratic lineage. He was a descendant of Rin Tin Tin. It appeared that a large, white collie had jumped over the fence where Rin Tin Tin was penned, or perhaps it was the other way around. At any rate, this is how Little Beast came to be among us.

Wind-of-Fire's and Little Beast's aunt was an extremely independent person. She and Brown Beast had worked out an arrangement of sorts in which neither imposed on each other's freedom. Brown Beast would show up to visit on occasion. I was an aunt to her too.

The neighborhood we were living in had a high crime rate. The apartment complex we lived in was one of the few in Chapel Hill that permitted pets. Brown Beast was beaten up by some of the kids in the neighborhood who were terrified of dogs and traveled through the apartment complex armed with knives and rocks. Wind-of-Fire was slashed over the eye. Brown Beast had compassion and Wind-of-Fire had a kind of sensitive integrity and empathy. But they definitely weren't "ladies" in the sense of having been sheltered from the world. Brown Beast was a matriarch, and Wind-of-Fire was on her way to becoming one.

Brown Beast seemed to understand Lady a lot better than I did, however. And it was only through Brown Beast that I came to terms with Lady at all. Because of Brown Beast's protectiveness and compassion towards Lady, I began to feel sympathy for her.

Little Beast had been teasing Lady ever since she came into the house. Brown Beast put an end to this with a gesture and look, both of which were implacably commanding. Little Beast stopped harassing Lady after that.

No doubt Brown Beast understood what Lady had been through. She understood the story of her abandonment. Probably she knew what the odds were also for Lady's future, how Lady could either be put to sleep or to death, not necessarily painlessly. Perhaps she also knew that Lady could be sold to the vivisectionists and tortured in a laboratory if we could not find a home for her. To my horror I was told, after leaving Chapel Hill, that animals that were unclaimed at the pound could be sold into laboratories for experimentation.

I had no idea what Lady was going through, her past or her realistic fears of the future. I didn't understand her desperation. She followed me around like a "wart," I harshly reflected at the time. Thank God we found what appeared to be a good home for Lady.

One day Brown Beast came to my house looking exhausted. It was late at night so I took Brown Beast upstairs and made a bed out of blankets for her and left her some food and water. Brown Beast accepted these things and lay down to rest. I felt blessed at being given an opportunity to be of service to Brown Beast. I admired the way Brown Beast led her life.

The Language of Untouchables

Wind-of-Fire and Little Beast have a passionate relationship. He gnaws on her ear continuously. When I come home from work, her ear is sopping wet. Little Beast wants to take Wind-of-Fire around with him to see the world. And all the world is Little Beast's. He is a sophisticated traveler and a Don Juan. Within a block away from the house, he forgets where he is.

One day Little Beast and Wind-of-Fire are playing outside the house. I see Little Beast head up the road. He turns around to Wind-of-Fire and gestures with his head, "Come-on." Little Beast is smart enough to avoid the dog catcher, but when he takes Wind-of-Fire with him, she ends up in the pound. After one such experience, I never let Wind-of-Fire out alone with Little Beast unless I'm with them both.

There's a little dog up the hill named Lelia who is Wind-of-Fire's rival. Little Beast, being the way he is, no longer having the companionship of Wind-of-Fire, picks Lelia up at the top of the hill. The two of them take off in full view of Wind-of-Fire who watches through the window of our house. Wind-of-Fire lets out a shriek of betrayal, and I let Little Beast know exactly what I think of him when he gets home.

The way Little Beast gets home, by the way, is by giving young women the impression he has rescued them, when in reality it is the other way around. In this he seems to have picked up one of the traits of a certain kind of male humanoid.

Little Beast goes up to the Chapel Hill campus where there are a lot of stray dogs. Some of these dogs are nasty to sweet and innocent female co-eds. Little Beast chooses a young and "helpless" co-ed when the nasty dogs are in sight, in spite of the fact they are not doing anything. He "guards" the co-ed from attack. The co-ed wonders where the owner of this Canine Knight in Shining Armor is, calls me and gives Little Beast a ride home, usually in an expensive car, praising his gallantry to the skies when they arrive at our doorstep.

In spite of his faithless ways, Little Beast is not at all unemotional about Wind-of-Fire. Wind-of-Fire is in heat and upstairs in our apartment duplex one day when a gang of male suitors from the top of the hill come down to weep and moan and cry. Since this gang is always attacking Little Beast, they don't have my sympathy.

Little Beast looks out the window and shrieks as loudly as Wind-of-Fire. He runs upstairs and humps her. Another tribute to his character that interest is aroused only in the presence of competition.

Untouchables do communicate with each other. They communicate with humans too. And I'm sure I have only touched on their language. It is possible to communicate with them, and to be aware of their communications with each other, from the very heart space that the scientists cut off when they imprison them as subjects for research, vivisecting their own brains, heart and soul in the process.

The Holy Spirit at Conception

Little Beast has been described as the only dog who could dent the fender of an automobile just by putting his paw on it. When Wind-of-Fire went into her first heat, I was summoned by her shrieks. Little Beast, who had managed to get inside Wind-of-Fire, was dragging her across the floor of the upstairs bedroom.

I had not planned to supervise what should have been an act of privacy and intimacy between the two. However, under the circumstances, I made Little Beast stand still. Wind-of-Fire stopped shrieking. And as things quieted down, I became aware of a presence.

Do I dare name the spirit I felt was present there? Should I call it Holy Spirit, Ruach, or any of the other names in many languages and religions and faiths by which the spirit has been named?

In orthodox Judaism, rituals were created to honor the presence of the spirit, Ruach, when two humans made love. There was the recognition that "making love," at least for the purpose of conception, was a holy act which involved the entire mystery of creation and life.

I'd experienced the spirit in several prayer groups. It was present in a poetry group I led in a health institute in Boston, to the surprise of an evangelical friend of mine. I've felt the spirit present in certain works of art. But I was surprised and awed by the presence of the spirit between two animals in the act of conception. No one had to teach them any ritual or prayers to invoke the spirit's presence.*

---

*In spite of the extraordinary quality of this experience, had I known what I do now about pet overpopulation and the cruelty and suffering animals endure as a result, I would have had Wind-of-Fire spayed before she had a litter.

The Birth of Twelve Puppies

I'm upstairs when Wind-of-Fire comes up to get me, apparently upset. She leads me downstairs, and I wonder what's going on. She settles in a large armchair. I sit next to her. I'm about to get up and go to work, but she communicates, "No, don't leave." So I stay. Then I see what's going on. Wind-of-Fire is giving birth. First one and then two little puppies come out. In all there are twelve.

One day Wind-of-Fire looks at me in desperation and communicates, "I can't take this anymore; too many puppies; not enough milk." I call a vet and she recommends weaning the puppies onto "puppy mush" for the rest of the nursing period.

A Saturn Tree

Wind-of-Fire lives and speaks the language of the psyche. Each day we take a walk in the woods near our house. There is only one tree in the woods whose leaves she likes to chew. The leaves are delicate. They look like miniature oak leaves, but I can't find out the name of the tree. The leaves hang on frail branches which fall over the path in the woods we walk on. A local herbalist says the tree is a Saturn tree. Saturn is the planet of responsibility. One day I discover what this means in terms of Wind-of-Fire.

Living the language of the psyche, Wind-of-Fire sometimes seems to move with a power beyond her own. I hear about two wild dogs, who live in the woods near our apartment complex, who have been attacking people. No one has been able to catch them. As Wind-of-Fire and I walk in the woods one day, with one of her puppies, two dogs approach us. I'm scared. I'm sure they're the dogs I've heard about.

First Wind-of-Fire chases one of the dogs out of the woods. She turns around and herds her puppy to safety. The other dog is making a beeline for me. But Wind-of-Fire is back in a flash and chases this second dog, cowering, out of the woods as well.

The Disappearance of Little Beast

Little Beast disappeared in the hills of North Carolina one day. I had given him back to his original "owner" because in the course of exercising him while I was riding my bike, he crossed in front of me and I ended up breaking my leg. To the member of the local fire department who observed this and who drove us home, before I made the trip to the hospital, Little Beast did not appear so gallant.

Little Beast's wandering ways did not end on his return to D. D. told his roommates to never let Little Beast outside without his tag and collar on, but one day they forgot. Little Beast left home without his tag and collar. No one saw him after that.

There are two other memories I will share about Little Beast, before we leave him for now. One day K., who owned a laundromat on the main street of Chapel Hill, said she was walking down the street when someone grabbed her and hugged her from behind. It was Little Beast.

Another time I was walking down this same street. There were two young men walking in front of me. I heard one say, "Did you see that?" The other said, "Yes." I looked in the direction they were looking in, and there was Little Beast literally jumping up and down for joy in the middle of the sidewalk and spinning around like a Sufi dancer or a Tevya on the roof.

Many in the town of Chapel Hill had gotten to know Little Beast before he disappeared that day. He was the "town clown" to some. Someone once offered me one hundred dollars for him. I told him Little Beast didn't have a price.

Dogs are He; Cats are She

I did not realize I had some negative feelings towards my own sex, though why I shouldn't when women have been so oppressed, I don't know. Most oppressed groups suffer from self-hatred at some stage.

When I was growing up I was, as mentioned previously, a "tomboy." I didn't identify with and despised a certain form of femininity which I identified as weakness. I hated the "weaklings" that women were raised to be.

I belonged to a girls' gang which performed feats like scaling rooftops and walking along the ledges of walls with steep drops beneath.

In a complex mixture of the ego and the divine, the streets of the lower-east-side of Manhattan provided another testing ground for me. I stared down young toughs shoulder to shoulder. I didn't consider myself violent when I socked a guy in the arm who felt my leg while I was climbing the stairs of the tenement where I lived. He was sitting with a group of men blocking my way. I said, "Don't you ever try that again." They never did.

I was proud of the fact that Yellow Jade was tough too. Most of the neighbors called Yellow Jade "he."

Dogs have come to represent the untamed part of men, while cats have come to represent the untamed part of women. In both cases, the real power of men and women is trivialized.

The power of men is reduced to the stereotype of a dirty, boisterous, haphazard animal. The dog becomes the embodiment of this projection. The woman who has identified with the obsessive-compulsive housecleaning role, her role as Keeper and Confiner of Matter, keeps male power under control through projections like these. In doing this she also confines herself. The real evil that is perpetuated on women by patriarchy is obscured and mystified by this trivialization.

With the cat we have an example of another projection. The cat is seen as an independent, picky, unfaithful, self-centered, spoiled, pest. Instead of cat, substitute women here. Anything that a woman wants, needs or does that takes her out of traditional and circumscribed roles, turns her into a pest. However, in this projection, female power is trivialized also. Domestic cats do not make lives for themselves; they are dependent on their human companions. Women who work and keep homes are hardly the frivolous, demanding objects this projection would imply.

In this projection of the unfaithful, independent woman in the portrayal of the cat, we see the fear of woman's power, the fear that women *will* establish their independence and rise above the role of "pet" or "pest." There is also the guilty knowledge that in some way many men have been complicit in making it difficult for women to become all they are capable of becoming.

Wind-of-Fire has never manifested any of the qualities of the so-called dog. Brown Beast, and other dogs I have known, have been dignified and hardly boisterous.

My cats Raynard, Courage and Moon, whose stories are

not told here, always followed me around the way only dogs are supposed to. They answered to their names and were and are the antithesis of the "fickle" and "faithless" cat.

However, this was not my thinking when I first got Yellow Jade. Like most speciesist humanoids, I called Yellow Jade "he" even though Yellow Jade was female.

Yellow Jade was as good a protector as any "he." Therefore I was proud of "him." "He" was a great watchdog. Even though "he" was small, "he" was no coward. I didn't realize that the pride I took in Yellow Jade had implicit in it a rejection of the feminine.

I initially admired Wind-of-Fire's warrior qualities. I remember her as a tiny puppy going from our apartment to the entrance of our building. Standing in the entrance she barked fiercely at the world, before she lost her nerve and ran back inside. That act of courage won my heart. I remember her when she was an older puppy barking fearlessly at a huge statue of a Confederate soldier on the campus of the University of North Carolina at Chapel Hill. She had no fear about chasing dogs, twice her size, including Dobermans, if they crossed her boundaries. And not only that, although she was a shepherd/collie mix, it was evident she was also part coyote. I believed this made her special and different. She had the dignity of the wild in her.

But as time went on I began to see her strength as something other than "toughness," as something other than the "warrior spirit." I began to see that these qualities have been equated with the "bravery" associated with "proving oneself."

So, when people called Wind-of-Fire "he," I would say, "No, she." I accepted and recognized the feminine part within myself as strong and something to be proud of and integrated what I had rejected previously.

An Indian on a Horse

It's 7.00 pm and I'm trying to meditate. I hear Wind-of-Fire panting. Panting is not entirely accurate. It's like she's having a seizure or being possessed.

At the same time I am startled by these sounds, I have an image of an Indian astride a horse beaming a light at me from the top of a hill.

Joan, Wind-of-Fire and Little Beast (left) in Chapel Hill

Basil (above) and
Yellow Jade (left)

Joan and Wind-of-Fire at seminary, 1981

Memorial Service for Wind-of-Fire, 1985. A universalist eucharist, *The Sharing of the Bread*, is offered to all present. [Photo above and photo on bottom of opposite page by Reginald Pearman/The Oakland Tribune.]

Blessing of the Animals of the Homeless,1991. Joan (right) blesses Kali and Flicka, the animal companions of Laura Bacon of Berkeley. [Photo by Karyn Radziner.]

St. Hubert, St. Basil and Basil

When a cross appeared between the antlers of a huge stag St. Hubert was about to shoot in a great forest of the Ardennes, he didn't try to get scientific proof of its existence. St. Hubert fell to his knees in awe. St. Hubert became the patron saint of the anti-hunters, who likewise did not question his vision of the gleaming, golden cross.

However, St. Hubert didn't live in the 20th century in which mystical visions are often relegated to pathology and only recently redeemed through explorations into extrasensory perception and parapsychology on the part of some scientists and researchers. Admittedly, it is difficult, if not impossible, to communicate a mystical experience in words.

I did not know about St. Hubert when I got involved with Basil. For that matter, I did not know about St. Basil either. I found the later to be named Basil near a gourmet food shop scrounging for something to eat one morning. My first response was shock at seeing such a beautiful, little puppy in such a plight. I tried to get someone to hold him while I called members of Friends of Domestic Animals in Berkeley to see if they could be of any help. None of them were home, and in the meantime Basil slipped away.

Later that day, I saw him again on the campus of the

81

University of California, Berkeley. This time he came over
to Wind-of-Fire who was unusually tolerant of him,
considering her low tolerance of puppies once she reached
maturity. Just as Basil, Wind-of-Fire and I were standing on
campus near a bank teller's window, synchronously, a man
came along and said that he owned Basil's mother. He had
given Basil away to a student a few weeks before.

The rest of the story is well-known. Students abandon
their pets in large numbers at the end of the school year. It
was summer when I found Basil; he was never reclaimed.

Basil was not toilet trained and was still teething when I
found him. I had not planned to spend most of my summer
taking care of Basil and trying to find him a home, but that's
the way it turned out.

Basil entered the formidable environment of the matriarch,
Wind-of-Fire, who at the age of five, and after twelve puppies,
made it known what her limits were. Basil became toilet
trained within a day when one night I tied him to the leg of a
desk so he would not teethe Wind-of-Fire and me to death. I
did not know that animals will not defecate in the area where
they sleep – logical of course. By the next morning Basil
was toilet trained.

However, there were other difficulties. I could not take
Basil with me everywhere I went and, after a week or two, I
found out that Basil barked continuously every time I left the
house. This had been reported to the manager of the building
by neighbors whose teeth were on edge. Basil could not be
left alone.

I received comments from some of my fellow seminarians

such as, "Joan, why don't you just take him out to the woods and leave him there?" Another said, "Why don't you just put him back out on the street?" A few admired Basil because he was golden, brisk, alert, with a half humorous, half wise, star quality smile.

In the weeks that followed, Basil met the humans who were a part of Wind-of-Fire's and my extended family. His family consisted of two grandmothers, one grandfather, one aunt and one uncle, who were a married couple. These dear people looked after Basil when I needed to do shopping or to leave him alone.

The summer I found Basil I had been trying to learn Hindu cooking. I was using an herb book. According to the book, basil was a good luck herb which the Hindus put in pots before their doors to ward off the evil spirits. A dictionary on names cited Basil Rathbone as an example of someone with the name Basil. Etymology told me that the name Basil comes from a word for "kingly." At that time, I also came across a quotation from St. Basil. St. Basil talked about the fact that the good deed we did not do was as much a sin as the evil deed we did do. That gave me comfort in the light of those who were suggesting I put Basil back out on the street.

For all of these reasons, I named Basil, Basil.

Later on, I discovered another quotation attributed to St. Basil. I did not think there were any members of the church with this perspective at the time St. Basil lived, in the fourth century common era, 330-379. As quoted, Basil, the Bishop of Caesarea, had written:

Wind-of-Fire

> *God, enlarge within us the sense of fellowship
> with all living things, our little brothers to
> whom Thou hast given this earth as their home
> in common with us ... May we realize that they
> live not for us alone, but for themselves, and for
> Thee, and that they love the sweetness of life
> even as we, and serve Thee better in their place
> than we in ours.*

The Return of Little Beast

"I do believe that animals reincarnate, and I could fill a book with stories to substantiate this belief. Love as a universal force is the energy which reunites souls on all levels."

　　　　　　　　　　　　　　　　- Dick Sutphen

Basil bore a remarkable physical resemblance to Little Beast. He chewed on Wind-of-Fire's ear in much the same way Little Beast had. This was quite a liberty if one knew Wind-of-Fire. When we went outside, passersby would comment:

"Why look at that dog chewing on that other dog's ear."

Some people I knew at the time thought of Basil as *my dog.* They would say:

*"Joan, when are you going to see he's **your** dog."*

Basil, when he came to Wind-of-Fire and me, looked like the beginning or end of another Little Beast. But he seemed to outgrow some of the Little Beast characteristics the longer he stayed with us.

Little Beast, as previously described, was an ecstatic as well as a Don Juan whose home was the entire universe. Basil seemed to sober up, but I always felt a great hilarity in him and that same ecstatic joy in him that was in Little Beast. Nevertheless, he was very loyal to Wind-of-Fire and to me, never wandered off and seemed to have more of a sense of being grounded in time and space. The only problem was his barking. I was afraid that if we didn't solve this problem, the first person who wanted him might bring him back or give him away.

Basil's two grandmothers and grandfather offered to send him to obedience school. I usually don't like the idea of obedience school, but this seemed like the best solution at the time. I knew the owner of an obedience school who had been a fellow seminarian. In the meantime I found some people who liked Basil and wanted to offer him a home.

During the summer I read a book about the spiritual journey of animals. It seemed to me in the time I knew Basil he had grown. My intuition told me that if Basil, indeed, had such a spiritual journey, that part of his journey on earth might be accomplished when he completed obedience school. For some reason I couldn't see him going with the people who wanted to offer him a home.

I was not surprised, therefore, to find out from the person who ran the obedience school that Basil had come down with distemper the day after he "graduated," apparently with flying colors. Basil had gotten his shots. Therefore, he must have gotten distemper from the streets before I found him.

The veterinarian recommended, after a few days, that he

be put to sleep. The distemper was getting worse and there was no possibility of recovery. I made the decision to have Basil put to sleep, and the veterinarian was surprised by my calm voice. However, I didn't feel that Basil's journey had ended with this experience on earth. And because of the intuition I had about him, I wasn't as upset as I might have been as a result of his passing.

However, within an hour or two of calling the veterinarian, I casually looked up at the ceiling and noticed a mass of swirling white light. I had never seen anything like this before. As I watched, the swirling white light opened up into a gleaming white cross. It stayed in that form for a few minutes, and then returned to the swirling white mass.

It took me a few minutes to get over the shock of seeing a cross on my ceiling. I went to the window and put up the blind to see if the light disappeared and it did. Then I took the blind down and there was the mass of swirling white light on my ceiling again. It didn't open up into a cross again. And after a while it disappeared. That was the only time in the apartment in which I had lived for almost a year that anything like that had ever happened. For that matter, it has never happened in my experience anyplace else.

Wind-of-Fire Receives Communion

"For when it [the lamb] heard the Brethren chanting in the choir, it too would enter the church, and, unbidden of any, would bend the knee, bleating before the altar of the Virgin Mother of the Lamb, as though it were fain to greet her."
                                        - St. Bonaventure

Last night there was a chapel service to celebrate the end of the *Fast for Life*. The *Fast for Life* participants, led by Dorothy Grenada and Charles Gray, fasted for forty days in the hope of bringing about a reduction of nuclear arms. I joined in with a support fast, emphasizing that nonhuman creatures also would benefit from a reduction of nuclear arms. This was the second fast I had done for animals. Some people supported my fasting for animals within the religious community, and I received anonymous notes from others who criticized my fasting for animals.

When individual testimonials were called for, I read my statement of support:

In my prayer period daily, I will include prayers for peace on the planet, an end to racism, sexism

88

and speciesism and an end to the dualistic
thinking that prevents us from experiencing a
unitive vision of ALL THAT IS.

Wind-of-Fire came with me to the chapel service, and when
the time came to receive communion, she got the bread and
I got the wine. I affirmed this as symbolic of the fact that all
creation is called to the "Lord's Supper."

Since then I have given communion to other animals, in
the same spirit. I gave communion to Aubrey shortly before
he died. For a long time I had had "a problem" with Aubrey.
When I went into Ed's tennis shop, I would pet Aubrey and
when I got ready to leave, Aubrey would go into spasms of
despair, howling and moaning. This happened so often that I
was afraid to have any contact with him at all.

Once I invited Ed to bring Aubrey to a *Blessing of the*
Animals service, but Ed was not a churchgoer, as he put it,
so Aubrey never came. However, one day I brought Aubrey
some bread that had been blessed for communion. After I
gave Aubrey the bread, there was peace between us. Aubrey
released me, to my relief. He never went into spasms of
anguish when I departed after that.

Eucharist and communion have not always been celebrated
as they are today. It is possible that what today is called
communion is based, at least in part, on an old Hebrew
religious ritual in which sacramental bread was given to those
in need.

Rarely do we find anything in the practice of communion
today that reminds believers of their obligation to serve the
needy, the outcast and deprived. The following quotation

by Ronald E. Osborn from *The Faith We Affirm* (St. Louis: The Bethany Press, 1979, p.62) is, therefore, unusual:

> *Our observance of the Lord's Supper as a covenant-sacrament expresses the fullness of our faith. By sharing at the Lord's table ... [we] affirm the oneness of Jesus Christ and ourselves with all who suffer, especially the oppressed, mistreated, and deprived (Matt.25:31- 46). The words 'broken body' and 'shed blood' remind us of God's presence as suffering love with all victims of the world's cruelty.*

The question is, *"How is this reminder of God's presence with those who are oppressed, suffer, are mistreated and deprived to be an active reminder?"* More often one gets the impression in an average church service that the communion being offered is for the elect, rather than for the outcasts, the least of these, among whom are the animals. I agree with Gandhi, when he said in his autobiography, *"I hold that the more helpless a creature, the more entitled it is to protection by man from the cruelty of man."*

When I hear in many churches, "This is my body broken for you," I do not get the impression that the Lord's body has been broken for abused, mistreated, tortured and suffering animals, or, for that matter, humans that are being mistreated and abused. I get the impression that the Lord's body has been broken only for certain individuals, who call themselves "Christians," who subscribe to a particular doctrine and are "saved." The universalist meaning of Eucharist has been totally lost in such rituals. And by offering the Eucharist, communion, to those who are outcasts, oppressed, mistreated, deprived, that more universalist meaning can be embodied. A truly cosmic universalist eucharist, for our time, must include all creatures.

I discuss the meaning of a universalist eucharist fully in my book *Creature Rites: Towards a Life Affirming Liturgy.*

In an excellent discussion of liturgy and rubrics, Sergei Fudel in *Light in the Darkness*, (Crestwood, New York: St. Vladimir's Seminary Press, 1989, pp.21-22), says:

> *Rubrics become dangerous when we forget that these are conditioned historically, when we dogmatize them....Freedom of love and rubrics can be brought together only when everything in one's own life stands at the right place: the absolute first, the relative second....Freedom and rubrics can be fused into one, only in true spirituality through the acquisition of the Holy Spirit....'If you are led by the Spirit, you are not under the law'(Ga 5:28), including church rubrics in the 'law.'*

In St. Basil's time, in the fourth century, according to Fudel, the eucharistic bread was given to the "faithful" who could keep it in their homes for the use of the sick.

Offering other creatures the eucharistic bread in our churches would be a great act of humility and an act of enlarging within ourselves our fellowship with all living creatures, as St. Basil asked us to do in his prayer. It would be a way of celebrating God's love of all creatures and an act of recognizing animals as the faithful of the faithful.

As Sergei Fudel writes, *"Formalism and sanctimoniousness is not Christianity."* Nor can *"external and dead action"* be the basis for any living faith.

I was discouraged from seeking ordination by individuals in one Christian denomination, the United Church of Christ, because of the fact I had given communion to nonhuman animals. It was suggested I write a paper about my theology of the sacraments. I presented this paper a few years later, and nobody that I am aware of bothered to read it; nor did anybody discuss it with me. I finally decided that I could not go along with the theology of the sacraments of this denomination, particularly its notion of "priestly ordination" based on administering the sacrament and withdrew.

At the end of the chapel service I swore inwardly to work in some way for animals as long as they are being abused, as long as I am on earth. The minute I made this vow, Wind-of-Fire let out a cry of ecstatic contentment.

Too Long A Name for a Dog

I have been told that Wind-of-Fire is too long a name for a dog. I am told that scientists have discovered that untouchables can only recognize the first syllable of their names. No doubt that is all Wind-of-Fire responds to.

Other humanoids seem annoyed that anything "lower" than a humanoid should be named with more than one syllable. Such a long name requires too much effort on their part for a mere untouchable.

While it is acceptable to say Alexandra, Anastasia, Angelica, Annunciata, Bathsheba, Benedicta, Catherine, Christabelle, Clarabelle, Clementine, Elizabeth, Ernestine, Esmeralda, Georgiana, Geraldine, Guinevere, Gwendolyn, Henrietta, Hildegarde, Jacqueline, Jeannette, Josephine, Persephone, Stephanie and Wilhelmina when these names belong to female humanoids and they prefer not having their names abbreviated, some humanoids feel it is a waste of breath to give names like these, or names of equal length, to an untouchable.

While one respects and does not abbreviate the names of male humanoids such as Alexander, Augustine, Bartholomew, Christopher, Constantine, Ferdinand, Frederick, Hildebrand, Huntingdon, Llewellyn, Maximilian, Nathaniel, Sebastian, Sutherland and Zedekiah when they wish to be fully named; surely one would not call an untouchable by a name like this, or equally long.

93

"What do you call her," people want to know.

"Wind-of-Fire," I reply.

"But what do your call her for short?"

*"Wind-of-Fire. It's sometimes the only line of poetry
I hear all day."*

Sue Browder in *The Pet Name Book* (New York: Workman Publishing Company, 1979) writes marvelously about the naming of pets. Browder gives many examples of generous, many syllabled naming of animals on the part of poets and writers. For example, Hans Christian Anderson in *The Ugly Duckling* named a hen Chickabiddy-Shortshanks. Thomas Carlyle "owned" a cat named Columbine. Christabel was the name of a poodle "owned" by James Thurber. Ferdinand is the name of the famous bull who refused to fight the matadors and preferred to smell the flowers in *The Story of Ferdinand* by Munro Leaf. Pyewacket is the name of the witch's Siamese cat in the movie, *Bell, Book & Candle.*

T.S. Eliot believed in many syllabled naming of cats. In "The Naming of Cats" (in *Old Possum's Book of Practical Cats*) he says that cats should have no less than three different names. Bombalurina, Jellylorum, Munkustrap, Growltiger, Lady Griddlebone, Bustopher Jones, Grumbuskin, Rum Tum Tugger and Jennyanydots are examples of names Eliot gives his cats in his poems.

Rudyard Kipling named a mongoose Rikki-tikki-tavi in *The Jungle Book*. Wilberforce is the three syllabled name of a remarkable pig in the book *Charlotte's Web* by E.B.White.

And there's Farley Mowat, who named a favorite wolf Angeline.

Naming Untouchables

I gave both "untouchables" the most beautiful names I could think of: *Yellow Jade* and *Wind-of-Fire*. I did not want their names to reflect either male or female qualities exclusively. In a world torn apart by dualities of all kinds, including sexism and speciesism, I wanted to emphasize the spirit they share with all forms of life. I named them with a vision of the future in which both sexes will value the characteristics labelled masculine and feminine and will discover and appreciate these qualities in themselves and others. Nonhuman animals will not bear the projections of either sex as stereotypes.

As a girl and as a woman I have been devalued as a result of the "outermost layer of my soul" being female and not male. I can, therefore, identify with other untouchables. I remember in my early twenties wanting to be identified and recognized as spirit so badly that I found human relationships painful, as most were so limited by stereotypes of being. I remember wanting and wishing there was somewhere I could take a vow of silence for years and years so I would not have to communicate in stereotypes. I didn't know at the time that this was not an uncommon practice for Hindu religious.

Yet the pain that animals feel for not being seen as spiritual beings must go unnamed. I feel the pain in the soul suffocated moans of a neighborhood dog tied on a chain for hours and hours at a time, like a prisoner in a dungeon, without any companionship and love. He is being seen as a rottweiler; in this case, he is being raised as an attack dog, one who is unfriendly to all strangers.

When he is still a puppy I am able to sneak him some food and water, a toy to play with. I talk to him and ease his pain and loneliness. He always greets me joyfully. His owners say that he is just young. He will learn to endure being tied up for hours and hours.

I never get a chance to help him more. When I am at the edge of indignation, when I can't bear his pain inside myself any longer as it is my pain too and my Creator's pain, the dog will no longer let me get near him. He barks at me. Shortly before they move, I watch his owners dragging him away on a leash as if he is some kind of a dangerous monster. I dissolve into tears for a long time. He is not that. Not that. Not that. As the Hindus say, to dissolve the illusions of the world, he is "not that." He has now forgotten who he is. I haven't. But there is nothing more I can do about it. I have not been able to name him truly for himself or others. And now, for him, it is too late. I hope in another time, another place, he will recover his true identity, reclaim a true name as a being who can give and receive love, with the same God given life in him as in all creatures.

The Naming of Wind-of-Fire

I have also been asked, "Why did you name her Wind-of-Fire?" Once I was asked, "Have you ever considered calling her, Wind-O'-Fire?" Some of the people in the apartment complex where we lived in Chapel Hill used to call her "Guinefire." They called Little Beast, "Wildebeast."

In answer to the question "Why did you name her Wind-of-Fire," I used to love the way she looked when she ran through the woods near our house when she was young. The redness of her coat and her swift motion through the trees made me think of a "Wind-of-Fire."

Wind-of-Fire's mother belonged to an astrologer who knew the birthdates of all the puppies. Wind-of-Fire was born on April 12, 1977. "Her sun is in Aries, a fire sign," the astrologer said. "Her moon is in Aquarius, a sign of air or wind."

The astrologer named Wind-of-Fire, Amanda. At the time I thought Amanda was an innocuous name. I did not know that the root meaning of the name Amanda is "worthy of love." So taking another route, I ended back in the same place. I named her Wind-of-Fire as a statement of her worth, the fact that she is significant and worthy of love -- not just her, but all others of her kind. I named her Wind-of-Fire as a way of saying that this creature is also in the image of the Divine; she is a worthy, beloved child of God/ess.

It is my prayer that we will all discover or rediscover the holiness of naming. Wind-of-Fire knew her name in her soul before it reached my lips. The minute I expressed her name, she came to me like a Wind-of-Fire, the way the Spirit has come to me at different times and places, unannounced -- Spirit of Life, Holy Spirit, Ruach. The same breath that breathes through Wind-of-Fire permeates the reality of this world.

> *Wind-of Fire, Holy Spirit, Ruach, Breath,*
> *Spirit of Life -- you translate into all forms*
> *of life and into all languages. You commu-*
> *nicate yourself through us in all forms and*
> *ways.*
>
> *You translate through Wind-of-Fire.*
>
> *You know her worth in you and through you*
> *when she is Feng Huo Gou, Fire-Wind Dog.*
>
> *You cherish her when she is Vent du le Feu.*
>
> *You manifest love through her when she is*
> *Ruach Shel Esch.*
>
> *And you cherish her when she is Feuerwind.*

She is worthy of love as Rih an-Nar.

And she is your beloved child as Vento di Fuoco and as Viento del Fuego.

She is possessed of your breath and your spirit as Tuuli Tuli, as Eldens Vind and as Vind Av Ild.

She is worthy of love as Aag ki Hawa and as Umoya Womlilo.

And she is your beloved child of great worth when she is Hinokaze.

There are those who would try to find a Wind-of-Fire, to touch it, consolidate it within a frame of comprehension. There are those who would dissect it, categorize it, despiritualize it, make it into a thing. There are those who would discover what unites things by tearing things apart, by separating things from themselves, by discovering what makes us different from one another, even if this means destroying us in the process. But we cannot be healed, helped or made whole in this way.

A Wind-of-Fire cannot be made into a thing. No one has ever seen a Wind-of-Fire. A Wind-of-Fire is a mystery. And those who try to tear apart this mystery, do so at their own peril. Ultimately, a Wind-of-Fire has no name.

Epilogue

Wind-of-Fire Passes On

Wind-of-Fire passed on, on February 12, 1985, Abraham Lincoln's birthday, from a pituitary tumor in her brain and from the world. Someone asked me what events were going on in Wind-of-Fire's life at the time she became ill. I took for granted that Wind-of-Fire was an emotional, physical and spiritual entity, having worked in the field of wholistic health. But I had not thought to examine what was occurring at the time Wind-of-Fire became ill.

"Joan, you aren't aware of the negative thoughts and energy that have been directed towards you and Wind-of-Fire as a result of your feelings for animals."

At first I wanted to pass her words off as morbid suggestions. This was a negative idea that was not to be looked at. Nevertheless, I looked.

I remembered one"graduation time" at the seminary. In high school yearbooks, students were elected the"most likely to succeed." The categories, anonymous seminary students had developed, included one that read "most likely to be crucified." For each category there were two choices. And Wind-of-Fire was chosen as one of the two most likely to be crucified. I remember staring in shock at the sheet of names. A student

I knew came along and said, "Didn't you know that people mutter about Wind-of-Fire under their breath?" "No, I hadn't known that," I said. "If they do, they have no reason to; Wind-of-Fire is a beautiful being."

Perhaps some day it will be shown that directing destructive thoughts towards others and backbiting can be as destructive, perhaps more so, than firing a gun.

Why did Wind-of-Fire become ill? And with a disease that couldn't be treated. A brain tumor. A rare occurrence in a dog, especially one of her age. When she was a puppy I thought I would feed her so well and treat her so well that she would go beyond her anticipated age span. And she died young. She would have been eight on April 12 the year that she died. The expression, "only the good die young" was certainly true in her case.

I now remember also the psychologist who interviewed me as a part of the process every seminarian had to go through to be ordained within the particular denomination I was considering at that time. She too said that she thought I was unaware of the degree of opposition to my theological beliefs concerning animals within the church and how I might be perceived as a result, the lack of acceptance I would encounter. In her written evaluation she said:

> *Joan is an independent thinker and visionary*
> *and many of her ideas, especially her passionate*
> *concern about animals and animal spirituality,*
> *may not be acceptable by others. She may be*
> *viewed by others as being 'eccentric' because of*
> *her unique views, and she may not be aware that*
> *she is perceived in this manner.*

I encountered opposition and roadblocks from members of the two denominations I attempted to work with, the Unitarian Universalists and United Church of Christ. I was told I was eccentric and a wave-maker by some of my fellow seminarians going for the ministry and the priesthood.

Rumors were spread at the seminary about Wind-of-Fire and me. When I brought Wind-of-Fire with me to one class that was held in the evening, a story was circulated that the instructor had to flea bomb his home as a result. The instructor was an animal lover, and he said the rumor was a total lie.

In one church in which I preached a sermon about animal rights which had nothing inflammatory in it, as far as I could see, I was told that there were members of that congregation who told the minister they would never come to hear one of my sermons again. What they considered inflammatory was the fact that I said, in my sermon, that a "church mouse" they planned to poison might be as valuable to God as the church building they were trying to preserve. Perhaps there was another way of getting the mouse out of the building without killing it. They had built the building, but God had "built" the mouse.

About a year later I discovered the book *Cathedral Mouse* by Kay Chorao (New York: E.P. Dutton, 1988). In this beautiful story a sculptor creates a little home for a mouse, out of stone, within a cathedral.

I was told by one Unitarian Universalist minister that if I wanted to work in the parish ministry and do an internship in his church, I would have to hide my animal rights commitment and appear to be a "moderate" in everything. He said it would be easier to be accepted as a gay person into the ministry than as an animal rights activist. No doubt he was just telling me "the truth."

I felt hopeful about doing an internship in another Unitarian Universalist church and was told by the minister that the internship committee considered my animal rights concerns a weakness. I thought of my concern for animals as a strength.

Another Unitarian Universalist minister told me that it was common knowledge in the parish ministry that if a minister gave a sermon that was considered at all "radical," one Sunday, he or she had better back off and give a "moderate" or even "conservative" sermon the following Sunday. He was being honest with me also.

For those who are familiar with the tarot cards, there is a card called the *Hanged Man*. It shows a man hanging upside down on a cross. This is the way I felt. Everything that was of value to me was obviously not of value to the churches I sought to work with.

In another Unitarian Universalist church I applied to do an internship in, the minister called me an extremist because of my views on animal rights and said the church was a church of moderates.

When I sounded out a member of the Unitarian Universalist Association in Boston about the possibility of being ordained to a community ministry in animal rights, I was told that it would be considered too "specialized" a ministry. I explained that my services were offered to people, also, who were grieving the losses of animal companions. Some services, such as the one I gave for people who lost their pets in the Berkeley/Oakland hills fire in California, also commemorated the wildlife. From my conversation with the member of the UUA, I definitely had the impression that my ministry wouldn't "fly" and that it would be a waste of time to pursue it with them any further.

Likewise, in spite of the individual support of Unitarian/ Universalists with whom I worked, none were able to find the support within their churches to ordain me to a special ministry that was, and is, inclusive of all creatures. "Congregational ordination" was discouraged by the denomination, I was told.

Having initiated the first resolution for religion and animal rights within Unitarian Universalism in 1984, I had great hopes that this denomination, reputed to be the denomination of progress and reform, would pave the way for others. A Unitarian Universalist minister who helped me draft this first resolution said it would take at least five years before it was passed. Fourteen years later, as of this writing in August, 1998, a resolution for Unitarian Universalism and animal rights has not been passed by the denomination.

I have been informed by individuals in the denomination that it is more difficult to get a resolution for animals passed, as it is not considered as important an issue as resolutions concerning humans. Unfortunately, it is this very humanocentric bias that may result in a planet in which it is no longer possible to be life affirming for any creature. My belief is that by truly embodying the interconnectedness of all life, a Unitarian Universalist "belief," by seeing life in other life forms as truly equal to life in one's own form, the good of all creatures will eventually become a reality.

Today animal rights activists who are abolitionists (against any research on nonhuman animals and against animal slavery in factory farms) are considered extremists. My views were not "moderate" enough for the Unitarian Universalists at the time I thought to become a parish minister or to have a special ministry in animal rights. The same pertained to my experiences with United Church of Christ.

However, it is interesting to discover that abolitionists of another cause, those who were totally against the enslavement of black people in America, also encountered opposition from their denominations.

I was astonished to discover that the Unitarian Universalists were not ready to embrace the cause of nonhuman animals as they have embraced other causes such as the rights of women. Historically, however, there are precedents for this.

According to Douglas C. Stange (*British Unitarians against American Slavery,* Cranbury, NJ: Associated University Presses, Inc., 1984, pp.17-18):

> *The Unitarian denomination has always esteemed a reform interest as one identifying characteristic of its membership .... This observation for the nineteenth century, however, is accurate only so far as the history of individual Unitarians is concerned .... [The American Unitarian Association (AUA)] was perturbed by radical reformers .... This was particularly true when some individual Unitarians campaigned against slavery in the 1830s.*

*They found their pleas for anti-slavery
pronouncements from their denomination
resisted .... By 1860, however, ...[the] antislavery cause was being proclaimed by nearly
everyone. Two Unitarian abolitionists who had
unsuccessfully pleaded with their denomination
to speak thirty years before, now were chosen to
draft an antislavery statement representative of
the denomination's newfound anti-slavery
consensus! .... The rejection and eventual
glorification by the AUA of the individual
American Unitarian abolitionists was essentially
duplicated by the Unitarian denomination in
Britain.*

Another denomination, the United Church of Christ (UCC), after many years finally passed a one-page resolution on *Respect for Animals* in 1993. The resolution raises questions such as, "Does the benefit gained from the use of animals outweigh the cost to them?"

A resolution that I helped some concerned rabbis formulate for the Northern California Board of Rabbis was so watered down when it "passed" that, in my estimation, it did little to protect or acknowledge the rights of animals.

In my experience, denominations are not in the vanguard of a cause such as animal rights, although individual members of denominations may be. As I discovered, even the most "progressive" denominations tend to be conservative when an issue of social justice is new and not at the stage where it is popularly accepted or supported. Some critics of organized religion go further and believe that particularly the western religious traditions, as practiced, have been a detriment to the rights of animals and the other creatures of the earth.

When I applied to one Clinical Pastoral Education (CPE) program, an internship in a hospital, which is a requirement for ordination in many denominations, I was asked by the pastor in charge if I was associated with the Animal Liberation Front (ALF). Would I be liberating or trying to liberate laboratory animals from the medical center. I told him that I was an abolitionist, against all research on animals, and I imagined there were others on the staff of the university medical center who felt the same way I did. (Another member of the committee questioning me acknowledged that there were.) However, I was not a member of the ALF. I realized after this discussion, however, that I would be "under suspicion" in any medical center that had a CPE program on its premises, if I revealed my beliefs about the rights of animals.

I did briefly enroll in a CPE program in which I worked with "underground" members of the hospital staff to find homes for feral cats that the administration wanted to destroy.

I was called a "prophet" by two ministers of United Church of Christ (UCC), the second denomination I tried to work with, as, among other reasons, UCC, at least theoretically, ordained individuals to special ministries. As the two ministers put it, "prophets aren't treated very nicely." Neither of them could imagine my making it through the ordination process, although one did offer his support at the same time he said, "Jesus never would have been ordained."

I was not unaffected by the atmosphere at the seminary involving incidents such as the "most-likely" one described above or the incidents that occurred in the process of my trying to get ordained to a parish and/or animal rights ministry. But I did not think of what this might mean in terms of Wind-of-Fire until I was asked what in fact was going on in our lives at the time her illness occurred.

I was told, while at the seminary, that there were trends within Christianity that included ecological ones, but I didn't see these trends being acted upon while I was there in regard to nonhuman animals. The environmental concerns seemed to be more like a "romantic umbrella," while the real issues never had to be dealt with personally and individually in one's own life. Not faced were the animals tortured in research laboratories. Not faced were the facts that seminarians, ministers and members of the church dined daily on the bodies of tortured factory farmed animals. Not faced were the facts that female ministers, seminarians and churchgoers, and even some of today's "progressive nuns," wore makeup that animals had been blinded for in cosmetics testing such as the Draize test.

The rainforests were far away. And concern for animals, except on the part of a few theologians, particularly those mentioned in the acknowledgments of this book, seemed equally remote. Any event or lecture organized by myself and, on one occasion, another person while I was at the seminary, were attended by one or two persons at the most. I was glad to see that one "event" was attended by the caretaker of the grounds of the seminary (who spoke mostly Spanish)

111

and a gay seminarian. I like to think that at least some individuals who have experienced prejudice because of their "differences" are more sensitive to others who are also being treated in an unworthy manner because they are "different."

In this case the organizer of the event, which involved the showing of a film of animals being abused in a laboratory, was from Finland. She couldn't believe that only two individuals showed up. I told her not to feel badly. This was the usual "quota" for such events. If no one had shown up or one person had shown up, the quota would have been beneath the norm. When I organized an event at a church, the "quota" was about the same. With very few exceptions ....

No one saw Jesus in the animals.

No one saw Christ in the cat with an arrow through its head chained in a laboratory, because no one wanted to look at pictures like that anyway.

No one saw Mary or God the Mother in the mother ape who had her arms protectively around her baby in a cage. They were both about to be separated and cruelly experimented on. No one wanted to look.

No one saw the Creator in the terrified animals with their arms around each other waiting in cages, aware of a terrible fate, about to be experimented on.

God wasn't supposed to be there. And if God was, this was of lesser importance than God being present in human victims of injustice.

God wasn't believed to be there in them!

Those who are among the most progressive members of the Christian community have assumed some collective responsibility in regard to what was done to the Jews in Nazi Germany. They have acknowledged the Christian contribution to anti-Semitism and the holocaust of humans. It is now time for denominations to do the same in regard to other forms of life. It is time to repent of destructive theological perspectives which lead to destructive thoughts and actions towards life forms unlike our own.

Yes, Jesus was in Wind-of-Fire.

Yes, Christ is in the animals.

Yes, God the Mother cares for them.

Yes, Mary was in Wind-of-Fire.

Yes, the Holy Spirit suffers in the animals.

Yes, the Creator suffers with the animals.

Wind-of-Fire

And Love was in Wind-of-Fire. And Love can respond to Love.

And that which was not of Love, and will never be, is no more with Wind-of-Fire.

On Leaving the Church

> *"The Goddess ... was a symbol of the unity*
> *of all life in nature. Her power was in water*
> *and stone, in tomb and cave, in animals and*
> *birds, snakes and fish, hills, trees and flowers ...*
> *This [Goddess] culture ... did not produce*
> *lethal weapons ... Their culture was a culture*
> *of art ... [the Goddess] ruled throughout the*
> *Paleolithic and Neolithic [in Europe] .... and*
> *now we find the Goddess reemerging from the*
> *forests and mountains ..."*
>
> - Marija Gimbutas

I have a dream about leaving the church. In the dream I am walking along a path, past fields of wildflowers, and I am one with the life force. The life force I am one with is the same as the life force in sun and flowers and all creatures of the Creator. I am not separate from Her.

It is Easter Sunday when I have this dream, and the dream is the celebration. In my dream, I walk past a priest dressed in black. He is leading his "flock" into an enclosed area and locking the gate behind them. I try to cover my breasts as I pass, realizing they are exposed. I realize the church is anti-life and anti-woman.

I come to my home and there's another priest, dressed in black, blocking the way to my room at the top of the stairs. I step around him and offer him a bright orange, a fragment of the life force. "Here," I say, "This is for you."

Then I turn away from him and go up to my room at the top of the stairs and go to sleep. And then, still in the dream, when I awake from sleep, I meet the Goddess in her many forms. She is combing my hair and doesn't want me to recognize her as she changes form, but I do anyway. She combs my hair as a bird and as a snake.

* * * * * * * * * * * * * * * * * * * *

On February 22, 1990, five years after Wind-of-Fire passed on of a pituitary brain tumor, I discovered I had one also. People asked me if there were carcinogens or toxins of some kind in an environment that both Wind-of-Fire and I shared.

In the years we were at the seminary together, Wind-of-Fire and I lived in four different seminary residences. It is possible that one of them was in a location that was too close to dangerously high electromagnetic fields from power lines. However, there were students who occupied these residences before we did and students who have occupied them since Wind-of-Fire and I left. Some of these students had pets, no doubt. I haven't heard of any other cases of brain tumors.

Before I got the tumor, I had never been ill with more than the common cold. In fact getting a cold was very unusual for me.

The only environment I could think of that was hazardous

to our health, that both Wind-of-Fire and I had been exposed to, was the *church*. What church doesn't matter. To me, any organized religious institution, including the individuals who are identified with it, which denies the spirituality of all creatures is the church to which I refer.

In my dream I leave that church and give it a farewell gift symbolized by the orange. It is a gift of my own life force which seemed to grow weaker over the years I made contact with the institutions, members and representatives of those institutions, that embody the anti-life, anti-nonhuman anima/l, anti-woman spirit.

The pituitary gland, in yoga and other mystical systems, relates to the sixth chakra, the third eye or center of one's spiritual understanding. My understanding that nonhuman anima/ls have souls and are to be cherished as children of one Creator was perpetually invalidated by the church over these years.

In early 1987, I began noticing some symptoms. Things got worse before the tumor was discovered. My fatigue was extreme, but worst of all, I felt I had lost my connection with God/ess. By the time the tumor was discovered, there was a part of me that wanted to die.

I lost my appetite for fruit. Fruit is the food that is closest to God/ess. When it is left to ripen and fall from a tree, it provides nourishment without harm to any living creature. My losing my appetite for fruit was a symbol of my losing my appetite for life.

After most of the pituitary tumor was removed in surgery, my appetite for fruit and life and my connection with God/ess returned. Every day since leaving the hospital I have eaten a couple of pieces of fruit a day. And the first piece of fruit I ate, after a three year abstinence, was an orange.

* * * * * * * * * * * * * * * * * * * *

I see a church where the nonhuman anima/ls with whom we share our lives, and those whose lives we do not intimately share, are celebrated.

I see a church in which the Creator is celebrated in the created, in dogs and cats, in horses and snakes, in rabbits, birds, squirrels, cows, monkeys, sheep, goats, elephants and all other creatures.

The birthdays of our anima/l companions are celebrated in this church.

The church finds sacred spaces where our anima/l friends can worship with us — outdoors and indoors.

I see a church in which memorial and remembrance services are offered for nonhuman anima/ls, the same way such services are offered for human anima/ls.

I see "baptisms" of nonhuman anima/ls, "welcoming ceremonies," in which the anima/ls are welcomed into the church.

Members of the church express their desire and commitment to care for these gifts of the Creator and ask for and receive support from other members of the church.

I see a church whose ministry will extend to nonhuman anima/ls. The church will seek shelter not only for homeless humans, but for the anima/l companions of the homeless and homeless anima/ls without human companions. The church will feed the hungry when they are nonhuman anima/ls, as well as the hungry when they are humans.

I see a church that will fight against oppression, infliction of pain, enslavement and cruel treatment of nonhuman anima/ls. The church will work to free the oppressed and offer sanctuary to "the least of these."

I see a church with one universalist eucharist reflecting the covenant and caring of the Creator with the entire creation. The universalist eucharist will be offered to creatures of the land, sea and air.

In the resurrected church, humans do not commit the "sin of ordination." Human and nonhuman anima/ls are welcomed into the ministry of the church.

Prior to surgery, I placed a fiery orange/red stone called a padparasha on my "third eye" and reflected on a "line of poetry," by Dane Rudyar, a friend had shared with me: *"Beneath snow-clad peaks a fire-worshipper is meditating."*

119

Wind-of-Fire

In my dreams, before the tumor was discovered, I saw snowcapped peaks and the world being frozen over with ice.

Wind-of-Fire. After the surgery, the orange/red fire of the spirit broke up the glaciation in my soul.

Memorial Service for Wind-of-Fire

(and all unmourned and suffering animals)

Two O'Clock , April 27, 1985
Berkeley, California

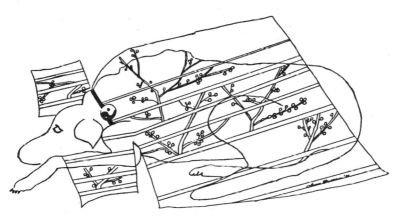

In Japanese, her name is Hinokaze

Order of Service

Callings   Paul Winter

Call to Worship

Leader: We gather together today to celebrate the death and resurrection of Wind-of-Fire.

People: And the death of all unmourned and suffering animals and their resurrection.

Leader: We gather together today to celebrate God's creation.

People: We believe all life is sacred and worthy of respect.

Leader: Our voices cannot be silenced to the destruction of the creation we see taking place.

People: We cry out for the coyotes and wolves, for the seal pups and cows, for the pigs and monkeys and dogs and all other animals who are victims of injustice.

ALL: It is a part of our faith and faith traditions to extend mercy and justice to all forms of life.

Invocation

Buddhist Prayer

Native American Prayer to the Four Directions of the Universe

Poem by Carter Heyward

WELCOME

The readings that follow are from *Animalia* by Barbara Berger (Millbrae, CA: Celestial Arts, 1982):

Reading from **"Little Brothers."** [St. Francis would remove small creatures, such as a snail, from the road out of harm's way.]

ALL: We ask that we may become more humble, in the spirit of St. Francis. May we uplift ourselves by "stooping" to care for the smallest creature.

Reading from **"A Choir."** [Brother Benno stopped his own prayers to listen to frogs "praying" in a swamp.]

ALL: May we be given the wisdom to listen less to our own voices and more to the voices of other creatures around us who "speak."

Reading from **"Happy Goldfish."** [A sage says he knows when fish are happy.]

ALL: We ask for the inspired reason of the heart so that we may be in better communion with the creatures around us.

Reading from **"Dream."** [A philosopher dreams he is a butterfly and is not sure whether he is a philosopher or a butterfly when he wakes up!]

ALL: May we be open to the Divine Mystery and recognize the transcendental nature of all forms of life.

Reading from **"Doves."** [A princess saves doves from being captured in a net.]

ALL: May we have the vulnerability to show our tears of compassion for suffering animals. May we have the courage to intercede for them.

Reading from **"The Stag."** [St. Godric saves a stag from hunters.]

ALL: We ask for the spirit of fearlessness and faith to protect all forms of life that are endangered.

Reading from **"Swan."** [Prince Siddhartha takes a swan from his cousin who has injured it. It is determined that the swan cannot belong to one who does it harm.]

ALL: We ask that animals only be in the hands of those who will not harm them, and we pray for their liberation.

Reading from **"The Turtle."** [A sage frees a large turtle from a trap. The turtle carries the sage across a river.]

ALL: May we be given the wisdom to recognize and honor more ancient forms of life than our own.

Scripture Reading:
>   *Old Testament*: Job 12:7-10
>   *New Testament*: Mark 6:15 (Oxford edition):
>> *"He said to them, 'Go into all the world and preach the gospel to the whole creation.' "*

Eulogy for Wind-of-Fire

Ringing of the Bells

Moment of Silence

Prayers of the Congregation

Pastoral Prayer:

>   *Prayer for all unmourned and suffering animals. Prayer for the bereaved who have lost*

*their animal friends. Prayer for all who work
for the rights and welfare of animals. Prayer
for those who are the enemies of animals.*

The Lord's Prayer.

Sharing of the Bread (A meal of agape for the creation.)

Velho Sermao (from *Common Ground* by Paul Winter)

Benediction

We welcome to our service of worship all who are visiting with us today. It is our sincere hope that all will experience a sense of God's presence in our midst and the grace that is extended to all of the creation. In honor of Wind-of-Fire, we cordially invite all to share a time of refreshment and conversation after the service. Out of respect for animals, only vegan food (food which does not contain any animal products) will be served.

Eulogy for Wind-of-Fire

She passed on just at the moment the flowers came into bloom, as if to spare me pain, knowing I would make the connection between her death and a new flowering of our friendship in God to come at a time of resurrection. The flowers coming out at the same time she passed, surrounded me with grace. I couldn't avoid seeing the evidence of new life.

I made a little memorial shrine to her and put flowers on the shrine to celebrate her spirit. I found a stem of yellow tiger lilies. One flower on the stem was in bloom when I brought it home. It died that night. The next morning, another had been born. I felt gratitude towards it for the continuation of life's spirit. As I embraced it with this thought, it moved gently. And, at another moment, the flower moved gently again, just as I was thinking of my loss of Wind-of-Fire. I used to call her Wind-of-Flower sometimes, and sometimes I called her Wind-of-Bird. I called her the Soul of the Universe. Wind-of-Fire was always able to care and see with her heart. When I was sad, Wind-of-Fire would come up to me wordlessly to comfort me and be there, a gentle, compassionate presence.

At the moment she passed, the words came to me, "it is complete." I had made her a purple velvet collar in her last days to be less abrasive on her neck which had lost almost all

127

its hair. I forgot to ask for the collar back when I took her body to be cremated. That was not complete. I needed to sew the threads of the unfinished parts of Wind-of-Fire's life and my life together down to what might appear like the very last thread. I had some purple cloth left and a handbag whose straps were badly tattered. So I made new straps out of the purple velvet cloth. With the last piece of cloth I made a sachet in which I sewed some herbs I had used to try to heal Wind-of-Fire. There was also an amethyst in the collar that had been lost. I had a set of keys which needed something on the key ring to distinguish that set from others. I bought another amethyst and fastened it to the ring. This was now complete.

In the days that followed, I put more flowers on Wind-of-Fire's memorial shrine. When I was a girl, I was an athlete and my nickname was *Lady Tiger.* The tiger lily always had special meaning to me. It also reflected Wind-of-Fire who was an athlete too. If someone threw a ball to Wind-of-Fire and her friends, she was the one who always caught it in midair. She never missed. I bought a dozen tiger lilies for Wind-of-Fire's memorial shrine to affirm her spirit of courage and daring. They bloomed and then their petals fell onto the floor. I let them stay there as Japanese gardeners let petals remain on the pavements without sweeping them away.

I decided to get some artificial flowers as a more permanent offering. I chose an artificial sprig of cherry blossom. I wanted to remember her in the spirit of the flowers of spring, in the joyous freshness and adventurous delight she took in life.

There was another unfinished part of Wind-of-Fire's life. We had often walked up the Fire Trail in Berkeley, but there was one part of the trail we had never gone into. It was always too late or too dark. In celebration of Wind-of-Fire, I took a walk with two of our friends, Yosha and Cynthia, up this trail.

Yosha loved Wind-of-Fire and always offered her his bones. We got to the part of the trail that Wind-of-Fire had always wanted to go down into. When Wind-of-Fire and I had reached this part of the trail, there were two barely perceptible paths leading off the main trail into the woods. Now someone had carved out these two paths that diverged from the main one in the form of a "V." Yosha, as if he knew just what to do, ran at breakneck speed down one arm of the "V" and up the other. "V," for victory we said.

Cynthia remembered Wind-of-Fire as having deep brown eyes that communicated exactly what she wanted to say. She told me that sometimes when I left Wind-of-Fire with her and she wasn't feeling good, Wind-of-Fire had comforted her. "She had an understanding of human emotions," Cynthia said. She remembered Wind-of-Fire as discerning, protective, nurturing, gentle and strong. Loving, sensitive and feeling were other words used to describe her.

Saiom wrote a poem to Wind-of-Fire which read:"*Fire kindled / Wind mingled / Light lingered / Soul soared.*"

A friend sent a photograph I'd forgotten about. It was a photograph I had taken of a tulip tree in spring. I remember how much fun Wind-of-Fire and I had when we went out to photograph the tulip trees together.

I had a hard time facing the fact that Wind-of-Fire would

pass on one day, years before she actually did. If you have ever loved another being, you can share my feelings with me. Wind-of-Fire was a miracle to me. I would look at her sometimes and not understand how such a miracle could ever pass. In terms of Wind-of-Fire, I could not understand death.

Towards the end I had to get her lab reports from a vet in North Carolina to find out the date Wind-of-Fire had been spayed. They didn't have the records anymore. The miracle that was Wind-of-Fire was no longer in existence in the vet reports in Chapel Hill, North Carolina. How could they not keep this important fragment of a miracle's life?

I don't know if Wind-of-Fire could accept her own death or transition. At the end it seemed like a great sadness came over her. I believe she knew about her illness a long time before I was ready to accept it or her moving on.

Christianity has been criticized as being the most insensitive religious tradition towards the animal world. In spite of this, there have always been Christians, as well as members of other religious traditions, who have cherished animals and who have been inclusive in their love for all forms of life.

I was fortunate to have, among my friends, some Christians like these at the time of Wind-of-Fire's passing, in addition to other friends, who gave me hope. They had not lost the deep intuitive sense that made it possible for them to believe that Wind-of-Fire and I would be reunited in another dimension of life. They had faith in what others had, unfortunately, "outgrown."

Some people were bewildered by my strong love for Wind-of-Fire. They didn't think a dog was worth that degree of attention or love. Others were moved to a new understanding of God's love for all of the creation through this witness.

We are brought up to believe that it is more favorable or meaningful if we discover God's love through another human being. If we are taught to seek God's love at all, we are rarely taught to see the potential of all forms of life to reveal that love to us. For those of us who have discovered God's love through an animal, we know that God's love is completely democratic. God doesn't have a hierarchy of love. Nor is God's expression of this love limited in terms of greater or lesser worth or value depending on the form through which that love is expressed. God isn't biased in regard to God's universe.

I had prayed that when Wind-of-Fire passed on she should be rewarded for the compassion she showed me in this life, the unconditional love she gave me and the expanded awareness of God's love for all the creation.

Had she left me in winter, in cold weather and rain, I might have seen no other possibility but death. But she left me in a season of natural and supernatural, to some, hope and resurrection. Lent and Passover, two occasions of triumph, were not far away when Wind-of-Fire left her body and rose to our Creator, lifted up by angels.

I remember the words from the memorial service of a human friend. The pastor said it was hard to understand why this friend had been taken away so young, but God had another ministry for him somewhere else. Wind-of-Fire died young too. She would have been eight years old on April 12 of the year she passed on. She died on February 12 of that year, on Abraham Lincoln's birthday. They say that only the good die young, and it certainly was true in her case.

Initially, it felt like an ironic twist of fate. When she was a puppy, I planned to feed her so well and treat her so well she would live to a much older age than the average dog. The opposite was true. I discovered "immortality" is a matter of one's perspective. I know God took Wind-of-Fire because she had a ministry somewhere else.

Postscript

Wind-of-Fire's memorial service was covered by *The Oakland Tribune* in its Sunday edition on April 28, 1985 under the headline, *"Creatures Great and Small Attend Rites for a Friend."* The reporter for *The Oakland Tribune* noted:

> *The pets [six dogs and one cat] were leashed and well-behaved, undisturbed by the tearful emotions that overtook some of the 25 animal rights activists who came to mourn the death of a dog named Wind-of-Fire and to support religious rights for animals.*

The reporter went on to say that the service *"... was graced by the solemn trappings of religion, including the sharing by animals and humans of a communion ritual. They took 'the bread of life,' served from a makeshift altar below the pulpit ... The animals took communion first, and some choked a bit on the 'bread of life' soaked in grape juice, but none barked or balked."*

The article also quoted a minister, who said he was ambivalent about the service and refused to attend, as saying: *" 'I don't think she is fully objective because of her grief, but she is not desecrating anything; quite the opposite, she is trying to make something sacred.' "*

After the service, I was informed that members of the Presbyterian church where the service was held believed the church had been taken over by "animal rights activists," the equivalent of a "dirty word." I was asked by the minister to come to the church the following Sunday. After the minister denied that "Christian communion" had been offered at his church, the congregation was informed that if they had any questions, they could direct them to me. Interestingly, no one seemed to have any questions to ask me, nor did anyone request to see a copy of the *Order of Service.*

Had they looked at the *Order of Service* they would have discovered that we did not call the sacrament "communion," but the *Sharing of the Bread*, with roots in the Jewish and Christian, matriarchal, Native American, and other religious traditions. Our universalist eucharist was communion, but not traditionalist Christian communion or the celebration of the Eucharist. We celebrated the Creator's covenant with all creatures in the universalist eucharist we offered.

One participant in the service had been doing an internship at a church prior to his ordination. He advised me that, as a result of the service, members of the congregation wanted to withdraw money from a fund for vestments they had set aside for him. I told him I'd be more than willing to talk with his congregation also if it would save his career. He said he didn't think that was necessary. Somehow the situation was resolved and the fund for his vestments restored.

One minister, who strongly objected to the "communion ritual," sent an article to me that appeared in *Monday Morning,* published by the Communications Unit of the Support Agency of the Presbyterian Church of America in New York City. He said he totally agreed with the article. The service was picked up by the *Associated Press* (AP) as well as *United Press International* (UPI), and apparently a Presbyterian minister had read about the service in a Virginia newspaper.

This minister, in the July 1985 edition of *Monday Morning,* said:

> *The central doctrine of the Christian faith is resurrection ....I read in a newspaper recently ... [about] a 'full-fledged funeral service' conducted in a Presbyterian church for Wind-of-Fire, 'a dog that died of a tumor' ... The object of the funeral service is the worship of God and the celebration of the promise of our resurrection because of Christ ... let us not sacrifice our faith upon the altar of humanism.*

In a biography of Anna Kingsford, a 19th century feminist mystic and animal rights activist, the author states that her last years were not happy ones:

> *Here, at the centre of institutional Christendom, she found that the Church had lost the supreme vision of the Christian faith — the deliverance of all creation ... 'into the glorious liberty of the children of God;' and that in place of this*

> *pristine splendour all that it could now see and*
> *teach was a selfish form of humanism —what*
> *human beings, here and hereafter and at*
> *whatever cost to the rest of life, must obtain*
> *for themselves alone.*

> \- John Vyvyan, *In Pity and in Anger*
> (London: Michael Joseph, 1969, p.151)

A couple of months later, the same minister, saying I probably would like this article better, sent me another article from the September 9, 1985 issue of *Monday Morning*. Another minister had responded to the first article about the service, saying:

> *The minister/author of the July '85 article in*
> Monday Morning *seemingly has problems with,*
> *the minister saying that God's love extends to*
> *all of creation, and offering prayers for animals*
> *that are victims of human injustice. I am*
> *disturbed by what this seems to say both about*
> *the role of a pastor toward a grieving person*
> *and about the relationship of humans to ani-*
> *mals ...There also is a danger in thinking of*
> *justice only in human terms as though we*
> *should live in just relationships with God and*
> *other people but the rest of creation is excluded*
> *from God's requirement of justice.*

There was no way of finding out where the service was reported unless someone told me. Among the newspapers which picked up the story from the *United Press International,* which came to my attention, I was glad to see the service reported in the *Japan Times*. The cremated remains of many animals are kept in Buddhist temples in Japan, and the priests say prayers for the departed animals. In fact, some Buddhists even have what they call an ordination ceremony for nonhuman animals in which they are welcomed into the community of Buddhists.

I was also glad to find out that Wind-of-Fire's memorial service was reported in the *Stars and Stripes* of the American Army. She deserved the farewell accorded to a heroine or hero. She had been a warrior dog throughout her life.

When we moved to California, however, something changed. She became more vulnerable. To my horror, Wind-of-Fire was often attacked by dogs, with and without their owners being present, on the streets of Berkeley. I was the one who came to her defense.

The warrior dog of physical territory became a "warrior dog" of the soul and spirit, fearless in love and compassion. She no longer defended boundaries, but was able to cross them into the heart.

In "prayer-talk-and-walk" I hope that we, the human species, may eventually find a way of living and being in a world with only boundless love for each other and all other creatures. In each heart, the lion and the lamb will lie down together.

About the Author

Joan Beth Clair is a theologian, educator, religious advocate for animals, a free lance writer, poet and artist. She holds a Master of Divinity degree and a Master of Arts degree in theology from the Pacific School of Religion in Berkeley, California.

Organizing and participating in workshops, panels and forums on religion and animal rights since 1985, Joan Clair has offered nonspeciesist religious services in the Bay Area and elsewhere, independently and as the founding director of Ministries for Animals. She has taught courses in religion in the Bay Area and is currently on the faculty of the University of Phoenix, San Jose, California.

Order Form

To buy more copies of **Wind-of-Fire: The Story of an Untouchable** ask your bookstore or order directly from **Wind-of-Fire Press**, PMB 1442A Walnut St. (173), Berkeley, California 94709, U.S.A.

Please send _____ copies of **Wind-of-Fire: The Story of an Untouchable** at $10.95 per copy to:

Name:_____

Address:_____

City:_____State:_____Zip:_____

Sales Tax: California residents please add applicable tax: 8.25% for books shipped to Alameda and Contra Costa counties, 8.50% for San Francisco and 7.25% for the rest of California.

Shipping: Book Rate: $2.00 for the first book and 75 cents for each additional book. (Surface shipping may take three to four weeks.) Air Mail: $3.50 per book.

Payment: Enclosed is my cheque _____, M.O. _____ for _____.

Fax: Attention: Wind-of-Fire Press, (510) 540-1057.